Freedom Roads

Freedom Roads

Searching for the Underground Railroad

Joyce Hansen and
Gary McGowan

Illustrations by James Ransome

Cricket Books
A Marcato Book
Chicago

Library of Congress Cataloging-in-Publication Data
Hansen, Joyce.
    Freedom roads : searching for the Underground Railroad / Joyce Hansen and Gary McGowan.—1st
ed.
            p. cm.
Includes bibliographical references and index.
        ISBN 0-8126-2673-7 (alk. paper)
    1. Underground railroad—Juvenile literature. 2. Fugitive slaves—United States—History—Juvenile
literature. 3. Fugitive slaves—United States—History—Sources—Juvenile literature. 4. African
Americans—History—Sources—Juvenile literature. 5. African Americans—Antiquities—Juvenile literature. 6. Antislavery movements—United States—History—Juvenile literature. 7. Antislavery movements—United States—History—Sources—Juvenile literature. 8. United States—History, Local—
Juvenile literature. 9. United States—Antiquities—Juvenile literature. 10. Excavations
(Archaeology)—United States—Juvenile literature. [1. Underground railroad. 2. Fugitive slaves.
3. Antislavery movements. 4. African Americans—History—Sources.] I. McGowan, Gary. II. Title.
    E450 .H26 2002
        973.7'115—dc21

                                                                                                    2002013711

To my aunts, Marilyn Williams Rivera and Gladys Williams. And to Jean E. Brown and Elaine C. Stephens for many years of friendship and support.—J. H.

To my family.—G. M.

Contents

Foreword

A century from now, when students and scholars want to know what life was like in the twentieth and twenty-first centuries, they will have many wonderful resources to help them re-create our history. Besides books, newspapers, magazines, and government documents, they will have film, video, audio recordings, and photographs. Not only will they see how we looked, but they will be able to hear how we talked. They will know what our music and what our twenty-first-century world sounded like.

When we research our recent past, for example, we can hear the moving voice of Dr. Martin Luther King, Jr., as he gave his famous "I have a dream" speech. We can see President John F. Kennedy sitting in the back of the limousine moments before he was tragically assassinated and his terrified wife scrambled in panic over the back of the car.

We can see the faces of pain and hear the cries of hunger from children around the globe—victims of war and famine. Because of modern technology, these and many other historical images have become part of our collective memory. The middle-school youngster and the middle-aged grandparent have, in a sense, witnessed the same history.

On the other hand, although we can read the touching words of President Abraham Lincoln's Gettysburg Address, we cannot hear him or see his facial expressions as we can with our modern presidents. Was his voice a high-pitched tenor or a deep bass? What kind of emotions were expressed in his eyes and tone as he gave that famous speech? We do not know and have only the information written by others. The further back we go in time the more difficult it is to know, and we can never know any historical period absolutely, even when we have lived through it.

Can you imagine, then, how difficult and almost impossible it must be to gather information about a time in our history when the activities of the men, women, and children who lived through it were purposely hidden?

The historical events that make up what is called "The Underground Railroad" are an example of such purposely hidden activities. It wasn't truly a railroad, but a series of secret escape routes

Sojourner Truth

leading enslaved people from bondage to freedom. Paths, trails, roads, and even waterways—especially waterways—were part of the "Railroad." "Underground" means that the activities were secret, and the words associated with a railroad—depots and stations—were the places where runaways could find assistance. Conductors were the people who sped them on their way.

Over time some of the stories about the Railroad have became romantic adventures with elements of myth and legend, and it is difficult to separate fact from fiction. How can we possibly find proof and evidence of activities that were purposely clandestine? Is there any way to recover a secret past? Perhaps.

The historian is almost like a detective solving a mystery. As a matter of fact, the detective and the historian have a lot in common. They are both concerned about the past. The detective has to research and re-create past events to solve a crime. He or she also has to delve into the history of the victim of a crime.

Like the detective, the historian has to research and dig for information to re-create bygone times. His or her goal is to help us understand as much as possible what a particular historical period was like. Where do we begin?

We start with the big picture and the things we already know. The history of the Underground Railroad is not only the story of fugitive slaves and abolitionists, it is also the history of America. As we search for clues about this hidden past, we begin by looking at the events that are documented in official records. Local and national laws are one source of historical evidence of the existence of an Underground Railroad. The laws that people create give us clues as to what is happening in a given society and reflect the concerns, fears, and goals of the lawmakers. The abundance of slave codes, for example—laws limiting the movement of enslaved people—is evidence that some men and women were running away, even when they had nowhere to run.

Legal petitions, court records, census records, and wanted posters can also give us evidence of Underground Railroad activity. Some of the most explicit physical descriptions of enslaved people are found in petitions and reward posters created by owners searching for runaways. To find the person, in those days before photographs and film, descriptions had to be graphic and detailed.

In addition to official records, sometimes even the mundane objects of everyday life can tell us about this hidden history—household records as well as plantation and farm records, bills of sale, receipts, ship registers, and information-wanted ads in old newspapers.

We can also learn from personal writings and accounts: biographies, autobiographies, memoirs, diaries, journals, and narratives of people who lived during the time of the Underground Railroad. Oral history, family history, narratives,

Frederick Douglass

and anecdotes about the activities of enslaved people, abolitionists, and ordinary folks who may have helped a runaway can all be useful in re-creating this era.

Music and art may also give proof of the existence of the Underground Railroad. Did spirituals and quilts contain hidden messages that aided runaways in their escape?

Modern historians have other tools now besides the traditional ones just mentioned. Archaeological research, together with historical documentation, can give us a picture of a specific time and place. It is surprising how much information the professional archaeologist can glean from an old button, a rusty coin, or a shard of broken pottery. Items that might seem useless to us can be a window into the past, verifying who lived in a particular place and when they lived there, giving us some idea of what their material world was like.

The Lott House

Our search for the Underground Railroad, then, will look at several archaeological sites where researchers have found possible evidence of Railroad activity. We will take this trip down freedom roads together and see whether we can find this hidden history. Although there may be some questions that we cannot answer absolutely, we hope to gain a deeper understanding about this period in American history, a time when individual people—slave and free, white, black, and others, rich and poor, well educated and illiterate—made personal choices that changed the course of our nation's history.

As we look at the roads and paths that led to freedom, our search doesn't begin with Pennsylvania Quakers aiding fugitive slaves; nor does it begin with homes and farms in Ohio and New York sheltering enslaved children, women, and men in secret tunnels and attics. The search begins in the oldest city in America—St. Augustine, Florida, and a nearby, almost forgotten Spanish fort.

Chapter 1

Running South
Artifacts from Fort Mose

St. Augustine, a quaint city on the northeastern coast of Florida, has unspoiled beaches and golf courses that are some of the best in the world. As far back as the 1880s, the city was a winter getaway for wealthy Northerners. They stayed at either the Alcazar or the Ponce de León, both luxury hotels. They enjoyed North Beach and Anastasia Island. Yacht racing was a favorite activity. The history of this city, however, stretches much further back than the late 1880s and is even richer than the luxury hotels and great golf courses.

In 1986 a team of historians, archaeologists, and scientists from the University of Florida conducted extensive research in order to rediscover an almost forgotten piece of this past. St. Augustine began as a Spanish settlement in 1565, when Spain laid claim to La Florida (Land of Flowers). It was the first European settlement in what would become the United States and remains the oldest city in North America.

The colonial records of Spain, Florida, and South Carolina give details about the settlement and the forts Spain built in the region to protect it. The research team, however, was interested in one fort and one community in particular, Gracia Real de Santa Teresa de Mose (moh-SAY). ("Mose" was a Native

American name; "Gracia Real" means that the town was chartered by the king of Spain; and "Teresa" refers to Teresa of Avila, the patron saint of Spain.)

The researchers were interested in this little-known settlement and fort, which in 1986 existed only on paper, because it was the first settlement of freed men and women in America. Fort Mose had been built and staffed by fugitive slaves from South Carolina in 1738 and rebuilt in 1752. Although it would be a challenge for the researchers, finding the actual site would bring back to life a history that was almost lost in time. Millions of Africans with families and personal histories, cultural traditions, ethnicities, and religions had become merely notations on a bill of sale or entries in a ship's ledger. They had been part of a ship's cargo—counted among kegs of rum and other goods. Through its artifacts, Fort Mose's people could speak for themselves—and expand our thinking about the Underground Railroad.

The first thing the research team had to do was to try to locate the fort's original site. Antique maps and descriptions of Fort Mose in the military and official records of Spain and South Carolina indicated the location. The settlement was composed of fields, where families living in the settlement farmed, and a small fort measuring "twenty meters square," built near a creek. The fort contained a well, a watchtower, and a guardhouse. James Oglethorpe, the British general who would launch a raid on the fort in 1740, reported to the South Carolina General Assembly that the fort had a "Ditch without on all Sides lined round with prickly Palmeto Royal."

When the researchers compared the old maps with the present-day surroundings, they discovered that the fort's original site had disappeared under a saltwater marsh. Through a process called *thermal imaging*, the archaeologists were able to locate the fort's ruins. Buried remains of buildings, foundations, and any other type of architecture exhibit fluctuations in temperature different from those of natural stone or streams. The archaeologists used instruments to measure these slight changes in heat distribution underground. Then they

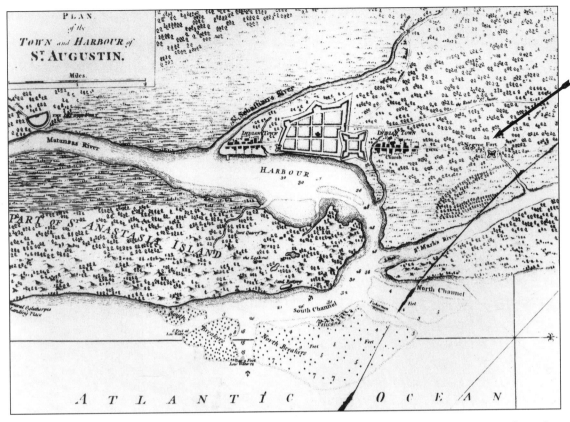

This eighteenth-century map drawn by Thomas Jefferys shows the town of St. Augustine and nearby Fort Mose in 1740. The words "Negroe Fort" can be seen on the far right-hand side of the map.

enhanced the outlines produced by the heat (thermal imaging) on a computer, and believed that they had found the vestiges of Fort Mose.

Because whatever remained of the fort was underwater, excavation was impossible, so the scientists began to search for the second Fort Mose. Once again, the team went to the old maps. A 1763 map showed that the second fort had been located near the original one, but as the team observed the islands and the marshlands, they saw no evidence that a structure had ever existed there.

Hope and Rebellion

The presence of a fort staffed by former slaves, many once owned by the British colonists, added to the colonists' fears of a slave revolt. But while Fort Mose was a symbol of rebellion for British slave owners, it was a sign of hope for slaves. The British colonists' fears of a slave uprising became real in the darkness of dawn on a Sunday morning on September 9, 1739. Twenty slaves met at the Stono River in St. Paul's Parish about twenty miles from Charleston. The rebels killed two men guarding a storehouse. They took guns and ammunition and proceeded to foment a slave rebellion in the area. Their band grew from twenty to fifty as other slaves joined them—some joined willingly, others were forced. The rebel slaves were captured as they headed toward St. Augustine in Spanish Florida. The following year, in 1740, General James Oglethorpe of Georgia attacked Fort Mose.

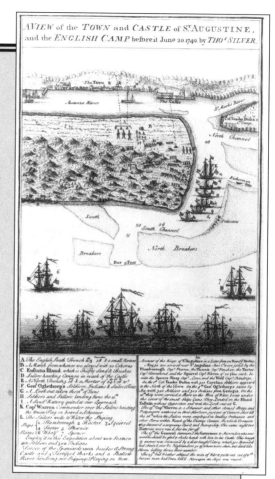

Thomas Silver's map depicts the events of 1740, when General James Oglethorpe of Georgia attacked Fort Mose and conducted raids into Spanish Florida.

Once again, the investigators turned to modern technology. After taking aerial photographs of the site shown on the 1763 map, they printed the photographs of the site at the same size as the map and then superimposed them on each other. The site of the fort as shown on the 1763 map turned out to be on an uninhabited small island in the marsh.

Luckily the island was not submerged under water. There was the possibility, then, that the archaeologists might be able to find the lost fort. They studied the island meticulously, looking for changes in the ground—often a clue that people had once been there.

By following special maps they had created showing changes in the land, along with the original maps of the fort and surrounding area, the archaeologists pinpointed the location of the original earthen walls. This was a great find. Soil is one of the most important elements in archaeological investigation. Often "soil stains"—discolorations—are the only indication of the remains of a building or structure. In the Fort Mose excavation, the moat that once surrounded the fort was identified by soil stains. The second Fort Mose was larger than the first, "65 meters to a side." The small, thatched-roof houses for the families were inside the fort. The fields that the residents farmed were outside the fort's walls.

Artifacts and remains found in the ground are often the "truth" of how people lived. They are different from an essay written from a personal perspective, or a diary written by an unreliable observer, or a book where some of the information is left out in order to create a certain perspective. An archaeological site, more than anything, can give us clues about how people lived. Depending on the condition and number of artifacts found, we can learn what kinds of foods people ate, what they wore, the type of work they performed, how they entertained themselves, how they worshiped, and in some cases, how they died.

The researchers carefully sifted the soil through fine-mesh screens so that even the smallest seed or tiniest bone fragment could be identified. The screens were also immersed in water to separate the particles of seed, bone, and plants from the soil. This process is called *flotation*.

What did the investigators find out about the runaways who manned the fort?

The artifacts suggest that the residents of the fort had only the basic necessities. Not in a position to accumulate many possessions, they were living on a rugged frontier and did not have an easy life.

Archaeologists found buttons made from animal bone, and thimbles and pins, showing us that people probably sewed and mended clothing. They found part of a tobacco pipe. Pottery shards, gunflints, and musket balls were also found at the site. The pottery was from cooking pots, and of course the artillery would have been part of the fort's arsenal. Some artifacts were related to religious life: a bead and a piece of woven metal might have been part of a rosary. They also found a St. Christopher's medal. Church records show that the Fort Mose residents had been baptized as Catholics.

Comparing official records with the artifacts helped the researchers analyze the significance of the items that were found. For instance, blue beads were unearthed at the site. From military, government, church, and other records kept about St. Augustine and the Fort Mose residents, it is clear that most of the residents were from West Africa or descended from West Africans. In some West African cultures blue beads were believed to ward off evil and illness. Most likely the people of Fort Mose, like other people of African descent in the New World, still held on to various aspects of their West African religious beliefs.

The soil samples revealed that people ate seafood and rabbit, deer, and other wild animals. An official report by one of the governors of St. Augustine confirms the archaeological findings. The governor reported that there was a good supply of fish and shellfish and that someday the Fort Mose settlers would grow food for themselves and for St. Augustine.

How do historical documents relate to what was found in the archaeological investigations? What can we learn about the fugitives who ran from the Carolina colony to St. Augustine?

In a 1687 letter to the king of Spain, the governor of the St. Augustine settlement, Diego de Quiroga, informed the officials in Spain that eight men, two women, and a three-year-old child had run away from the South Carolina colony and sought refuge in St. Augustine. One of the men, Mingo, had escaped

The area between Charleston, South Carolina, and St. Augustine, Florida, giving some idea of the coastal route escapees from South Carolina may have taken

with his wife and daughter—the three-year-old child. The governor told the officials in Spain that the fugitives wanted to be baptized in the "True Faith."

The runaways had arrived by boat, probably a canoe, which would have been the only way to travel through the swamps, creeks, and inlets from South Carolina to Florida. We can't begin to imagine what a harrowing trip that must have been, especially with a young child.

Papers of William Dunlop in the South Carolina Historical Society archives confirm the residents' escape. In 1688 Major Dunlop was sent on a mission to St. Augustine. In a letter to Major Dunlop dated June 15 of that year, Governor James Colleton listed all of the tasks that Dunlop was to perform on his mission, including, "You are likewise to demand the delivery up to you of those English fugitive Negroes and others [possibly white indentured servants] who have fled from this province."

How did the eleven Carolina slaves reach Florida? They may have escaped in 1686 when their settlement on Edisto Island was raided and burned down by Spanish pirates. Someone must have aided them—otherwise how would they know that St. Augustine was a place to escape to? How did they find their way? And how did they know that they should ask to be baptized in the Catholic faith? Like any underground operation, that was a secret. Perhaps one of the men in the group had been to St. Augustine with his owner. If so, he would have seen that there were blacks in the settlement who were free. He might have been told that if he converted to Catholicism and agreed to be baptized, he would be freed. Or maybe a Native American who had dealings with the Spanish and didn't care for the British helped the group get to St. Augustine. Maybe a fellow slave in Carolina told one of the runaways about St. Augustine and explained how to get there.

The Seminoles

When Florida became an English colony in 1763, it continued to be a refuge for Native American and black runaways. The secret paths that had been used earlier to reach Florida from the Carolinas and Georgia remained for those who were brave and daring enough to run. Runaway slaves reaching Florida allied themselves with various Native American groups called Seminoles. ("Seminole" comes from the Spanish word *cimarrón,* meaning "maroon" or "runaway.") In 1816 and again in 1835, black and Indian Seminoles, resisting removal to the West, fought against the U.S. army. The fascinating history of the black Seminole Indians is set in Florida, Oklahoma, Texas, and Mexico during the eighteenth and nineteenth centuries. Their struggle to escape to freedom, often across the border to Mexico, parallels the struggles of the black men and women who were running to the North.

In a 1688 written agreement between Major William Dunlop and the Spanish governor of St. Augustine, Dunlop confirmed that the runaways "are turned Roman Catholick Christians" and would stay in Florida, and that the British would be paid for their value.

Historical documents show that other fugitives from the Carolina colony would find their way through the forests and swamps to St. Augustine. In 1693, the Spanish crown issued a royal proclamation offering refuge to slaves who reached St. Augustine and agreed to be baptized. The fugitives would be under the protection of the Spaniards as long as they remained in St. Augustine. The officials in the colony would not return them to South Carolina, and the South Carolina colonists could not march into St. Augustine and claim their slaves. Florida was Spanish territory, and Spain was not going to return valuable slave property to its enemies.

As the Carolina colony grew from its small beginnings in 1670, its presence rankled the Spanish authorities in Florida. From their perspective, a British colony so close to Florida was a bold challenge to their colonies in the Caribbean and their territory in Mexico.

The close proximity of St. Augustine to the Carolina colony is reflected in the correspondence and official records between England and its colony. In response to a question about St. Augustine from officials in London in 1719, for example, the South Carolina Assembly replied that the only trade or enterprise the Spanish had was making pitch and tar with the help of black slaves stolen "by their Indians from our frontier Settlements."

In a letter dated 1720, a resident of the Carolina colony wrote that officials had uncovered a plot by slaves to take over the colony and kill all of the white

> ## Slave Laws in the Colonies
>
> Spanish laws regarding slaves were based on codes dating back to the thirteenth century that gave enslaved people certain rights. Slaves could own property and buy their freedom, and they could be granted freedom as a reward for contributions to the state. Male slaves, for example, who joined slave militias or served on Spanish vessels could be freed. Families were kept together; slaves could sue a master because of ill treatment; slaves were baptized and allowed to marry in and join the church. Whether or not these laws were enforced was left to the officials who interpreted and administered the law. Church records, however, give evidence that to some extent enslaved men and women in St. Augustine and other Spanish colonies might have fared a little better than their counterparts in English colonies.

inhabitants. The writer notes that "some of the slaves involved in the plot tried to get to St. Augustine and to get some Creek Indians to show them the way."

Whether there really was a plot is uncertain, but the Spanish in St. Augustine had been using Africans and Indians in their colonial militias, which may have unnerved the Carolina colony. Some of the male slaves who escaped from South Carolina helped defend the city when it was attacked by the British in 1728.

Fugitives from Carolina continued to make their way to Florida, and in 1733 Spain declared that after four years of service to the king, they would be given their freedom papers. For the men and women who had escaped South Carolina, this probably seemed like trading one slave master for another. They continued to press the Spanish authorities for total freedom, but it wasn't forthcoming until 1737, when the colony was assigned a new governor.

By 1738, when there were more than a hundred refugees from South Carolina living in St. Augustine, Governor Manuel de Montiano removed them and established the Fort Mose settlement. Thirty-eight families lived there. In 1740 the fort was attacked and badly damaged by English forces, and the town's residents were removed to St. Augustine for safety.

For the next twelve years the Fort Mose residents lived in St. Augustine as free people. They worked there among free and enslaved Africans from various countries and colonies, Native Americans, and Spanish citizens. Parish records of the St. Augustine Cathedral include baptism papers and marriage certificates showing that many of the Carolina refugees married one another. Some also married Indians and whites. Interracial marriages were customary in the Spanish colonies, as were marriages between free and enslaved people.

Fort Mose was rebuilt in 1752 and remained a community of freed men and women. The census records of 1759 list twenty-two thatched houses in the settlement; the residents included thirty-seven men, fifteen women, seven boys, and eight girls. By then not only could enslaved men and women in South

Carolina look to the St. Augustine settlement as a means of escape, but they also had Fort Mose as a beacon of freedom. The Fort Mose settlement remained a free black community until 1763, when Florida was ceded to the British after the French and Indian War. The residents of Fort Mose, however, left with other Florida colonists and resettled in Cuba in Matanzas Province.

Their history, then, would continue in another country; yet they left a legacy of self-emancipation that would grow as slavery became entrenched in the Southern colonies.

Chapter 2

Land of the Free
History in a Ship's Log

If you made regular trips to busy New York Harbor in Manhattan from April through November in the year 1783, you would have noticed a number of black men, women, and children boarding the British frigates, sloops, brigs, and schooners leaving the port.

You would have seen infants in their mothers' arms as well as children ten, eleven, and twelve years old. Some of the older boys and girls would have appeared to be alone, whereas others were traveling with an adult. You would have also spotted many young men and women in their twenties and thirties who seemed to be healthy and strong, along with people in their forties and fifties and some older than that.

And among all of the people you would have seen, whether young or old, male or female, some would have seemed tired and sickly. You might also have seen several inspectors board a vessel to make sure that the British were not taking any American property, including slaves, with them. After the ship was inspected and papers signed, it set sail, leaving New York, bound for Canada and Europe.

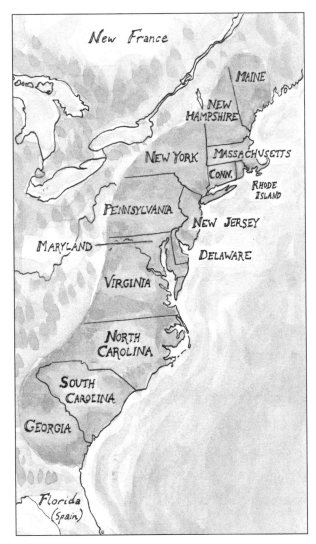

Map of the thirteen British colonies

For many of the black passengers, the voyage would be the beginning of a new life as free people. When the British evacuated New York City after the War of Independence, a total of three thousand black men, women, and children left with them.

During the war, the British military had offered freedom to any slave or indentured servant who helped the Crown put down the American rebellion. The black passengers, running away to the British lines, cast their lot with the Crown. Some enslaved people followed the roads and waterways that led to the British regiments and naval vessels.

In chapter 1, we saw how archaeological artifacts and modern technology can provide clues to the history of the Underground Railroad. In this chapter and the next, we will begin to see how certain kinds of paper evidence can add to that knowledge. Through runaway notices and articles in newspapers found in colonial archives, through military records in the United States and Great Britain, and also through personal and official correspondence, journal entries, and personal narratives, we can piece together the history of the black men and women who attained freedom by finding their way to the English forces during the Revolutionary War.

Some of the most interesting and surprising pieces of evidence reflecting the experiences of black people who escaped to the British lines are the inspection rolls (embarkation lists) of the British ships that left New York Harbor in a seven-month period in 1783. Of the three thousand people of African descent named on the rolls, 1,336 were men, 914 were women, and 750 were children.

The lists note the name of each ship, the ship's master (captain), and the destination of the vessel. Most important, the rolls give the names and ages of the individual travelers, including short comments and sketchy physical descriptions. They also include the names of people who formerly owned the passengers, as well as the names of people who claimed to own them.

As part of the peace negotiations at the end of the war, General George Washington

A page from the inspection rolls of a British ship leaving New York in 1783

insisted that Americans trying to retrieve their slave property be given a hearing. Sir Guy Carlton, the British commander-in-chief, established a board of inquiry to hear the cases of Americans trying to reclaim their slaves.

The board met once a week at Fraunces Tavern, a historic New York City restaurant that still exists in present-day lower Manhattan. Carlton, however, tried to protect the black men, women, and children who had responded to the British promises of freedom if they left their "rebel" masters. Those who had entered the British military ranks before 1782 and had loyally served the military for the remainder of the war received certificates for transport out of the country.

General Washington also required that he receive information on every black man, woman, and child leaving with the British evacuations so that Americans could make future demands for reparations for lost property in slaves.

American officials inspected each ship and its black passengers and signed off on the inspection rolls. There were times when people were taken off the ships and brought before the inquiry board—if, say, a former owner insisted on reclaiming an enslaved man or woman who had run away to the English troops.

It is one thing to read the name and age of someone on a list, but when there is even a slight history or the barest sketch of a description, the person becomes a little more real to us. The rolls and the entries are witnesses to this tumultuous time and to the individual choices that people made to try to free themselves. The following entry is from the collection of ships' inspection rolls of April 23 to September 13, 1783:

> Name of Ship: Aurora
> Where bound: St. John's
> Passenger: Billy Williams
> Age: 35 years old
> Description: healthy, stout man
> Person claiming ownership of Billy Williams: Richard Browne
> Remarks: Formerly lived with Mr. Moore of Reedy Island, South Carolina, from whence he came with the 71st Regiment about 3 years ago.

This entry shows several things. Although Richard Browne is claiming to be Billy Williams's owner, Williams left or escaped from a Mr. Moore. Williams, like so many other enslaved people, especially those who were skilled workers, may have been bound out to Moore, but was Browne's slave. Moore would pay Browne for the work that Williams performed. It is noted that Williams had joined the 71st Regiment three years earlier, which would have been when the

British occupied Charleston in 1780. Also, he is described as healthy and stout—the kind of man who could be of service to the military.

Correspondence dated June 1782 between the British commander-in-chief and his aides supports the fact that some slaves served the British forces ably. Carlton was told that some blacks "have been very useful, both at the Siege of Savannah and here [Charleston], some of them have been guides and from their loyalty have been promised their freedom."

> ### Freedom with the British
>
> Perhaps as many as 65,000 Southern slaves left their owners and fled to the British. A historian writing in 1858 stated that South Carolina lost two-thirds of its enslaved laborers to the British military. Some historians estimate that from 80,000 to 100,000 men, women, and children left with the British evacuation at the end of the war; not all, however, were freed.

Other entries not only reflect the events of this period but give us some idea of the complexity of the slave system and the people caught up in it. In a number of entries people claim to be freeborn, yet they are still leaving the country. According to the agreement between the United States and Britain, the English were not supposed to carry off any man, woman, or child who belonged to someone else. Perhaps some of the people claiming to be free were not. The only way for them to escape reenslavement was to leave the country.

Some people were indeed free, but freedom for blacks was tenuous and uncertain. Free blacks had very limited rights, and the only way they could live as full citizens was to leave the country.

The descriptions in all of the entries are very subjective. Some of the adjectives used would be insulting to us today. Women and girls are repeatedly referred to as "wenches." Sometimes a person is described as "an ordinary looking fellow," "a likely boy," "a fine child," or "a squat little man." The majority of the entries described people as "stout," meaning strong and sturdy, which makes sense. To run away and offer your services to the military, you would most likely have to be young and strong.

Name of Ship: Nancy

Where bound: Halifax

Passenger: Ursula Fortune

Age: 24 years old

Description: Stout wench

Person claiming ownership of Ursula Fortune: Captain Frazer Guideste

Remarks: Says she was born free, served her time with Mr. Benjamin
Hubbert nigh Fredericksburg, Virginia.

Ship: Jane

Where bound: Port Roseway

Passenger: Tom Davis

Age: 25 years

Description: stout make [*sic*]

Person claiming ownership: John King

Remarks: Says he served with Phil Tygner, Cumberland County,
Virginia. Says he is no slave; left his master 5 years past.

Ship: Sally

Where bound: River St. John's

Passenger: John Primus

Age: 22

Description: stout fellow

Person claiming ownership: William Bell

Remarks: Says he is born free and produces a Certificate dated 29
July 82 from Robert Ballingall, Commissioner of claims at
Charlestown; he is hired as a Sailor on board.

Ship: L'Abondance

Where bound: Port Roseway

Passenger: Judith Wallis

Age: 2 weeks

Description: healthy infant

Remarks: Daughter to Margaret Willus; born within the British lines

Ship: Apollo

Where bound: Port Roseway

Passenger: Chloe Crumline

Age: 45 years

Description: Old and worn out

Person claiming ownership: George Patten

Remarks: Formerly slave to Harry Crumline, Santee, South Carolina;
    left him 5 years past

Passenger: Prince Wigsal

Age: 25 years

Description: Short and stout

Person claiming ownership: Richard Whittin

Remarks: Formerly slave to Mr. Wigfall, Charlestown; left him at the
    Siege of that place.

Ship: New Blessings

Where bound: Portsmouth

Captain: Thomas Craven

Remarks: The mate declared there was not any Negroes or American
    property of any kind on board

How did this exodus to the British lines begin? Through regimental records, as well as personal and official correspondence, we can see how the Revolutionary War provided a means of escape for enslaved people. Volunteering for military service had been one way of gaining freedom in the past. During the French and Indian War (1754–1763), for example, colonial militias overcame their reluctance to arm black people and enlisted men of African descent when recruiters could not get enough white soldiers. After the French and Indian War some black soldiers received their freedom.

As soon as the War for Independence began, black men joined colonial militias, fighting at Lexington and Concord on April 19, 1775, and two months later at the Battle of Bunker Hill. The Belknaps of Framingham, Massachusetts, freed their slave, Peter Salem, so that he could enlist in the militia and help the patriots' cause. The muster rolls of one New Hampshire regiment listed three black men. They were described as "effective, able bodied men, but they are slaves enlisted with the consent of their master."

The Continental Army, organized in June, would not enlist slaves or free blacks. Officers feared that the army would become a refuge for runaways who claimed to be free. After three years of fighting and shortages of manpower, however, the army changed its policy. As enlistees grew scarce, some recruiters did not bother to ask many questions about a man's status. If he was strong and able-bodied and claimed to be free, then he was accepted.

Only Georgia and South Carolina refused to enlist black soldiers into their regiments. One scholar has estimated that because the American military did not want black men in the Continental Army, only about five thousand African Americans fought on the patriots' side during the war.

In 1775, when the members of Parliament in London realized that the colonists in America were more than a "rude rabble" protesting high taxes and unfair laws, they searched for ways to quiet the growing rebellion. On November 7, 1775, John Murray, Earl of Dunmore, the royal governor of Virginia, issued a proclamation declaring "all indented [indentured] Servants, Negroes, or others . . . free, that are able and willing to bear Arms, they joining His Majesty's Troops."

By His Excellency the Right Honorable JOHN Earl of DUNMORE, His Majesty's Lieutenant and Governor General of the Colony and Dominion of Virginia, and Vice Admiral of the far,&c.

A PROCLAMATION.

AS I have ever entertained Hopes, that an Accommodation might have taken Place between GREAT-BRITAIN and this Colony, without being compelled by my Duty to this most disagreeable but now absolutely necessary Step, rendered so by a Body of armed Men unlawfully assembled, firing on His Majesty's Tenders, and the formation of an Army, and that Army now on their March to attack His Majesty's Troops and destroy the well disposed Subjects of this Colony. To defeat such treasonable Purposes, and that all such Traitors, and their Abettors, may be brought to Justice, and that the Peace, and good Order of this Colony may be again restored, which the ordinary Course of the Civil Law is unable to effect; I have thought fit to issue this my Proclamation, hereby declaring, that until the aforesaid good Purposes can be obtained, I do in Virtue of the Power and Authority to ME given, by His Majesty, determine to execute Martial Law, and cause the same to be executed throughout this Colony: and to the end that Peace and good Order may the sooner be restored, I do require every Person capable of bearing Arms, to resort to His Majesty's STANDARD, or be looked upon as Traitors to His Majesty's Crown and Government, and thereby become liable to the Penalty the Law inflicts upon such Offences; such as forfeiture of Life, confiscation of Lands, &c. &c. And I do hereby further declare all indented Servants, Negroes, or others, (appertaining to Rebels,) free that are able and willing to bear Arms, they joining His Majesty's Troops as soon as may be, for the more speedily reducing this Colony to a proper Sense of their Duty, to His Majesty's Crown and Dignity. I do further order, and require, all His Majesty's Liege Subjects, to retain their Quitrents, or any other Taxes due or that may become due, in their own Custody, till such Time as Peace may be again restored to this at present most unhappy Country, or demanded of them for their former salutary Purposes, by Officers properly authorised to receive the same.

GIVEN under my Hand on board the Ship WILLIAM, off Norfolk, the 7th Day of NOVEMBER, in the SIXTEENTH Year of His Majesty's Reign.

DUNMORE.

(GOD save the KING.)

John, Earl of Dunmore, issued this proclamation on November 7, 1775, offering freedom to indentured servants and slaves who joined "His Majesty's Troops." This offer of freedom, however, applied only to enslaved men and women who belonged to colonists rebelling against British rule.

Parliament had come to the same conclusion as the Spanish back in 1733, when the king of Spain issued his edict offering asylum to runaways. The British realized that the massive desertion of slave labor to their lines would destroy the Southern economy and weaken the patriots as they struggled to hold together their plantations and their military forces.

Southerners were horrified over the Dunmore proclamation, especially in Georgia and South Carolina, where blacks outnumbered whites. The Virginia colony wasted no time in preparing for the possibility of slaves attempting to reach Lord Dunmore. Officials established what were called "home front" procedures, increasing slave patrols and warning people to be aware of slaves trying to steal small boats to escape to the governor's fleet. Maryland also guarded its shores to keep blacks and indentured servants from boarding a British warship on the Potowmack (now Potomac) River.

Newspaper articles, diaries, and correspondence of this period note incidents of slaves trying to escape to Lord Dunmore's fleet. Rumors flew that slaves were "stampeding to Lord Dunmore's ships." Perhaps this statement was an exaggeration as panic spread among the Virginia patriots. A couple of weeks after the Dunmore proclamation a group of slaves was captured on the James River as they attempted to reach Dunmore's ships anchored off Norfolk, Virginia. Thirteen slaves in Northampton, Virginia, were sentenced to death for stealing a schooner and attempting to sail it to the

Escape

In a diary entry written on Wednesday, June 26, 1776, Colonel Landon Carter of Virginia described a well-planned escape by his slaves. "Last night after going to bed, Moses, my son's man, Joe, Billy, Postillion, John, Mullatto, Peter, Tom, Panticove, Manuel & Lancaster Sam, ran away, to be sure, to Ld. Dunmore, for they got privately into Beale's room before dark & took out my son's gun & one I had there, took out of his drawer . . . all his ammunition, . . . Landon's bag of bullets and all the Powder, and went off in my Petty Auger [water craft] . . . and it is supposed that Mr. Robinson's People are gone with them, for a skow they came down in is, it seems, at my landing. These accursed villains have stolen Landon's silver buckles, George's shirts, Tom Parker's new waistcoat & breeches."

James River. Seven black men escaped from a Virginia jail, stole a canoe, and made their way to Lord Dunmore. When Dunmore's fleet sailed out of Virginia in August 1776, about three hundred black people left with them. They would serve in the British military.

As the entries in the inspection rolls show, a number of women also made the attempt to reach the military. A newspaper article in the December 20, 1775, *Pennsylvania Gazette* reported that nine slaves, two of them women, were captured as they tried to reach Norfolk.

During the fall and winter of 1775, blacks who reached Dunmore's ships were mostly strong, healthy men who worked as soldiers, seamen, and laborers. The fugitives were especially useful as pilots because they knew the waterways in the tidewater region of Virginia. Some became servants to British officers. There was also a place for women who found their way to the British lines; they worked as laundresses, servants, and cooks.

In 1784 a census was taken among some of the men who had left with the British. Over two hundred of them had settled in Birchtown, Nova Scotia. There were "forty-six carpenters, thirty-seven sawyers and eleven coopers. Thirty-five black refugees were sailors, ship carpenters, rope makers, caulkers, blacksmiths, barbers, cooks, bakers, shoemakers, tailors and chimney-sweeps." This gives us an idea of the kind of work that many of the refugees had performed in the American colonies. Many of these jobs were useful to the military.

Despite the risk of being captured and punished for running away, a number of slaves seized the moment and tried to escape to the British lines. This time, they had a real and definite place to run to. The fugitives left no records of how they escaped or who helped them. No doubt, fellow slaves aided in these flights.

As the war continued, British generals issued more proclamations to the slaves of American rebels. In 1780, for example, when a fleet of British warships anchored on the Cooper River near Charleston, South Carolina, slaves from nearby plantations made their way to the ships. John Ball, a South Carolina

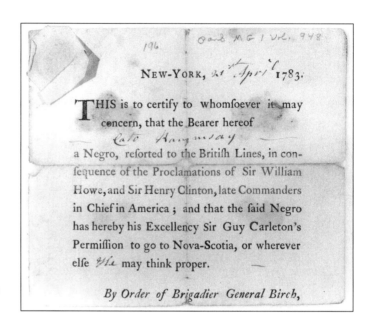

NEW-YORK, 21st April 1783.

THIS is to certify to whomfoever it may concern, that the Bearer hereof *Cato Ramsay* a Negro, reforted to the Britifh Lines, in confequence of the Proclamations of Sir William Howe, and Sir Henry Clinton, late Commanders in Chief in America; and that the faid Negro has hereby his Excellency Sir Guy Carleton's Permiffion to go to Nova-Scotia, or wherever elfe *fhe* may think proper. ——

By Order of Brigadier General Birch,

A copy of the certificate of freedom that the British generals gave to the African Americans who left with them at the end of the Revolutionary War

slave owner, kept a day-to-day list of slaves on his plantation who ran after the Union Jack.

> May 7—Toby gone to the [British] camp, & Hyde Park Abraham.
>
> 9th—Phoebe & her daughter Chloe
>
> 10th—Charlotte, Bessy & her children, Roebuck, January, & Betty
>
> 11th—Yamma
>
> 12th—Patra & daughter Julia
>
> 13th—Flora & child Adonis
>
> June 1st—Pino went in my flat [boat] and carried with him his wife Nancy, Little Nancy, Polly, Dick, Jewel, Little Pino, Nanny and child Nelly, Peter, Eleanor, Isabel, Joney, Brutus, Charlotte.
>
> June 2nd—Humphrey

In one of the South Carolina low country (southern coastal region) parishes, a planter stated that one-half of the adult male slaves had left their plantations to follow the British military and never returned. For these slaves, like the slaves in Virginia, inlets and rivers were the "roads" that led to freedom.

Unfortunately, few of the people who evacuated with the British were able to leave a written narrative of their experiences. Narratives do not offer the same kind of historical evidence as government or military records because they are told from one person's point of view, but when a narrative corresponds to what we know historically, it gives us an insider's look at the past. The following narrative, written by Boston King in 1798, takes us back to the Revolutionary War period and into the heart and mind of a slave who had freed himself.

Memoirs of the Life of Boston King, a Black Preacher, Written by Himself, during his Residence at Kingswood School

I was born in the Province of South Carolina, 28 miles from Charles-Town [Charleston]. My father was stolen away from Africa when he was young. I have reason to believe that he lived in the fear and love of God. He was beloved by his master, and had the charge of the Plantation as a driver for many years.

My mother was employed chiefly in attending up those that were sick, having some of knowledge of . . . herbs, which she learned from the Indians. She likewise had the care of making the people's clothes, and on those accounts was indulged with many privileges which the rest of the slaves were not.

When I was six years old I waited in the house upon my mother. In my 9th year I was put to mind the cattle. . . . When 16 years old, I was bound apprentice to a trade. After being in the shop about two years, I had the charge of my master's tools, which being very good, were often used by the men, if I happened to be out of the way: When this was the case, or any of them were lost . . . my master beat me severely, striking me upon the head, or any other part without mercy.

One time in the holy-days, my master and men being from home, . . . the house was broke open, and robbed of many valuable articles, thro' the negligence of the apprentice who had then the charge of it. . . . The week following, when the master came to town, I was beat in a most unmerciful manner, so that I was not able to do anything for a fortnight.

About eight months after we were employed in building a store-house, and nails were very dear at that time, it being in the American war [Revolutionary War], so that the work-men had their nails weighed out to them; on this account they made the younger apprentices watch the nails while they were at dinner. It being my lot one day to take care of them which I did till an apprentice returned to his work, and then went to dine. In the mean time he took away all the nails belonging to one of the journeymen, and he being of a very violent temper, accused me to the master with stealing of them. For this offence I was beat and tortured most cruelly, and was laid up three weeks before I was able to do any work. . . .

My proprietor [owner], hearing of the bad usage I received, came to town and severely reprimanded my master [Mr. Waters, the man to whom Boston was apprenticed] for beating me in such a manner . . . the two succeeding years, I began to acquire a proper knowledge of my trade. My master being apprehensive that Charles-Town was in danger on account of the war, removed into the country, about 38 miles off. . . . Having obtained leave one day to see my parents, who lived about 12 miles off, and it being later before I could go, I was obliged to borrow one of Mr. Waters's horses; but a servant of my master's, took the horse from me . . . and stayed two or three days longer than he ought. . . . I expected the severest punishment, because the gentleman to whom the horse belonged was a very bad man, and knew not how to shew mercy. To escape his cruelty, I determined to go to Charles-Town, and throw myself into the hands of the English. They received me readily, and I began to feel the happiness of liberty of which I knew nothing before, altho' I was much grieved at first, to be obliged to leave my friends, and reside among strangers. In this situation I was seized with the smallpox, and suffered great hardships . . . by the blessing of the Lord I began to recover. . . .

Being recovered, I marched with the army. . . . Our regiment had an engagement with the Americans. . . . But our situation was very precarious, and we expected to be made prisoners every day; for the Americans had 1600 men, not far off; whereas our whole number amounted only to 250: But there were 1200 English about 30 miles off; only we knew not how to inform them of our danger, as the Americans were in possession of the country. . . .

Soon after I went to Charles-Town and entered on board a man of war. . . . We were going to Chesepeak-bay. . . . We stayed in the bay two days, and then sailed for New-York, where I went on shore. . . .

Boston King was among those who left New York with the British and headed to Canada. He lived in Nova Scotia for five years and then relocated to Sierra Leone, where he became a schoolmaster. His entry reads as follows:

July 31, 1783

Ship: L'Abondance

Where bound: Port Roseway

Passenger: Boston King

Age: 23 years old

Description: Stout fellow

Remarks: Formerly the property of Richard Waring of Charlestown, South Carolina; left him 4 years ago.

Chapter 3

A More Perfect Union
Learning from the Law

The laws and ordinances governing a nation, state, city, or even public and private institutions can be a window into the past. Laws tell us as much about the people who wrote them as about the society that lawmakers wanted to fashion and sustain. Laws are similar to the kinds of physical evidence we saw in chapter 1 in that they have many layers of interpretation.

For instance, Congress passed the Fugitive Slave Act in 1793, allowing a slave owner or his agent to capture a fugitive and go before a U.S. circuit or district judge or even a local magistrate in the county or state where the slave was seized. The owner would have to present an affidavit from a judge in the state the fugitive had fled, certifying that the runaway was his or her slave. Anyone trying to help a known fugitive would be fined five hundred dollars, a great sum of money in those days.

We learn some basic facts from the existence of this law. Because many of the Northern states were in the process of abolishing slavery by 1793, enslaved people had more places to run to. Indirectly from the law, we might conclude that so many more people were escaping and running away in the years after the end of the American Revolution that slave owners pressed for a law to strengthen the article in the Constitution that referred to runaway slaves.

When we look at just a few laws, going back to colonial times, we can see that some applied to enslaved men and women who ran away. As early as 1643, Massachusetts and Connecticut included in their Articles of Confederation a law regarding the return of runaway servants (indentured servants or slaves) to their masters. The person claiming the servant needed only a certificate from a magistrate in his or her jurisdiction to have the servant returned.

A 1705 law in the records of the General Assembly of New York forbids slaves from "travelling forty miles above the city of Albany, at or above a place called Sarachtoge [Saratoga], on pain of death," if they were not with their owners.

So here we see another road leading to possible freedom. Since a law was passed against slaves traveling this way alone, there must have been a good number who attempted it, perhaps in order to find refuge among Native Americans.

Looking at the laws and rules of private and religious organizations also gives us an idea of past antislavery activity. The Society of Friends, also called the Quakers, was among the first religious organizations to take a firm stand against slavery. The Quakers' beliefs and their own religious oppression led them to practice abolitionism long before it became a widespread cause. As early as 1688 the Quakers of Germantown, Pennsylvania, spoke out against slavery at their weekly meeting: "Is there any that would be done or handled at this manner? . . . Now, tho they are black, we cannot conceive there is more liberty to have them slaves, as it is to have other white ones. There is a saying, that we shall doe to all men like as we will be done ourselves; making no difference of what generation, descent or colour they are. And those who steal or robb men, and those who buy or purchase them, are they not all alike?"

Not all Quakers followed the wishes of the Germantown Meeting, and in 1696 at their yearly meeting the Germantown Friends issued a stronger statement: "That Friends be careful not to encourage the bringing in of anymore Negroes." This injunction against slavery was repeated in stronger terms over the years. Quakers were encouraged to free their slaves, many believing that anyone who professed to be a Quaker could not be involved in importing, selling, or buying slaves. By 1776, it became compulsory among the Quakers of Pennsylvania that any who had slaves free them.

Judging by the regulations of the Society of Friends, we can surmise that the Quakers influenced the laws enacted by the State of Pennsylvania and can understand why in 1780 Pennsylvania was first among the states to enact a law allowing for the gradual abolition of slavery. Slaves from Maryland and Delaware would eventually find the roads that led to Pennsylvania. In the meantime, the delegates to the Constitutional Convention would also gather in Pennsylvania to create the laws that would hold the new nation together after the War for Independence.

> ### A Single Bead
>
>
>
> As we saw in chapter 1, what is found buried in the earth offers its own documentation of historical events. A chevron bead found in an excavation of the home of Caleb Cresson of Philadelphia, Pennsylvania, has been identified by archaeologists as an African American artifact. The Cresson family were prominent merchants and Quakers in Philadelphia. James and Joshua Cresson signed a 1783 antislavery petition at their yearly Philadelphia Meeting. The identification of the bead and other African American artifacts indicates that most likely the Cresson family employed black workers who lived on the family property. Some of these workers could very well have been former fugitive slaves who managed to escape into Philadelphia and were aided by certain Quaker families.

From May to September 1787, George Washington of Virginia, Alexander Hamilton of New York, Charles Pinckney of South Carolina, Roger Sherman of Connecticut, Benjamin Franklin of Pennsylvania, and fifty-one other delegates to the Constitutional Convention met in Philadelphia.

These men had the difficult task of developing thirteen former British colonies, loosely held together by the Articles of Confederation, into a solid nation with a central government. The government had to be strong enough to form the individual states into a union, while at the same time allowing each state to function according to its own needs.

William Penn

It was fitting in a sense that the Constitutional Convention was held in the former colony of Pennsylvania. Its founder, William Penn, was a Quaker espousing a doctrine of tolerance long before the Founding Fathers met in Philadelphia in 1787. Penn, born into a wealthy English family in 1644, was twenty-two years old when he became a Quaker. At that time in England the Quakers were an oppressed and scorned religious sect. Penn was jailed because of his religious beliefs, but continued preaching the Quaker doctrine of religious tolerance. In 1681 King Charles II gave Penn a land grant in North America which became Pennsylvania ("Penn's woods"). In 1682 when William Penn visited the colony, he made treaties that were considered fair and just with the Delawares, Shawnees, and other indigenous people in his colony. In a letter to Native Americans in the

colony he wrote, "I have already taken care that none of my people wrong you, by good laws I have provided for that purpose." Over the years, Pennsylvania would become the destination of many enslaved men and women seeking freedom.

From the White Mountains of New Hampshire to the rice and cotton plantations of South Carolina and Georgia, there was such a wide variety of physical environments, economies, and cultures that the former colonies, now states, were almost like separate nations. The Constitution would have to be flexible enough to join them together as one.

Unfortunately, the War for Independence, while freeing the American colonists from British rule, did not free the slaves within the new nation. And the Constitution, the great body of laws that still forms the foundation of American government and democracy, did not abolish slavery either.

The organization of Congress, the duties and powers of the presidency, the structure of the federal courts, and many other concerns important to the fragile new nation were debated and discussed. But on the issue of slavery, there was a loud silence. Yet, whether the delegates wanted to debate the issue or not, it remained like an uninvited dinner guest and had to be acknowledged.

In the debates from May 14 to June 19 that dealt with representation and taxation, the question of population arose. Would Indians, slaves, and indentured servants be counted as part of a state's population? Would Southern states with large numbers of slaves end up with more representatives in Congress, giving them greater power than smaller, less populated states? The wording of Article I, Section 2, of the Constitution settles the issue without ever using the word "slave":

> *Representatives and direct taxes shall be apportioned among the . . . states . . . according to their respective numbers, which shall be determined by adding to the whole number of free persons, including those bound to service for a term of years and excluding Indians not taxed, three-fifths of all other persons.*

The "three-fifths of all other persons" were the enslaved population. This clause is often referred to as the "three-fifths compromise."

By Tuesday, August 22, the uncomfortable issue of slavery could not be held off any longer. The delegates tried to limit the focus to the slave trade and whether to import new slaves into the country. They told themselves that since some states had already begun to abolish slavery, if the importation of slaves into the United States could be halted, then slavery within the nation would eventually be eliminated by attrition.

Luther Martin, a Maryland delegate, stated that trading in slaves contradicted the principles of the Revolution and dishonored "the American character." Another delegate warned that "the crime of slavery might yet bring the judgment of God on the nation." Some delegates wanted to know how they could condemn the slave trade and at the same time not abolish slavery within the country.

John Rutledge did not accept the argument about religion and humanity: "It was a matter of 'interest' alone." It was a matter of economics. Slavery was the foundation of the Southern economy. Thousands of slaves had been lost during the war. Charles Pinckney and other delegates from South Carolina and Georgia asserted that they could not agree to laws that banned the slave trade and thus hindered their ability to import slaves and acquire the necessary labor needed to make their plantations productive. One South Carolina delegate reminded the others that the slave trade was beneficial to the Northern states as well, providing goods, produce, and business opportunities for Northern merchants. A Connecticut delegate agreed. "What enriches a part enriches the whole," he said.

Roger Sherman, who signed both the Declaration of Independence and the Constitution, said that "it [was] better to let the Southern States import slaves than to part with those States." Another Connecticut delegate, in words that give the impression that he was annoyed with the whole slavery debate and wanted to move on, said that each state should be allowed to make its own decision about the "morality" of slavery: "Let every State 'import what it pleases.'"

Perhaps the business interests won out in the end. The delegates from South Carolina and Georgia refused to sign the proposed Constitution if it banned the importation of slaves. The large rice and cotton plantations were entirely dependent on slave labor. From the most skilled artisans such as carpenters and blacksmiths to experienced agricultural laborers and household servants, slaves performed all of the work.

The rest of the delegates did not want to lose these two states. And perhaps the comment that ultimately voiced the truth was "What enriches a part enriches the whole." The slave trade debate ended two days later when the delegates settled the issue in Article I, Section 9:

The migration or importation of such persons as any of the states now existing shall think proper to admit shall not be prohibited by the Congress prior to the year one thousand eight hundred and eight, but a tax or duty may be imposed on such importation, not exceeding ten dollars for each person.

"Such importation" refers to slavery. Until the year 1808 the states that wished to do so would be allowed to import slaves into the country. This would give the slave states twenty-one years to import all of the slave labor they needed; domestic slavery would not be abolished. Some of the delegates thought that it would just die a natural death if slaves were no longer imported into the country.

Whereas the first two laws we looked at were compromises with the Southern states, doing nothing to end slavery but instead weaving it tightly into the fabric of the nation, Article IV, Section 2, reflects another issue in the slavery debate:

No person held to service or labour in one state, under the laws thereof, escaping into another, shall, in consequence of any law or regulation therein, be discharged from such service or labour, but shall be delivered up on claim of the party to whom such service or labour may be due.

This statement reflects more than anything the reality of slaves trying to free themselves. "Person held to service or labour" refers to slaves. Article IV is an indication that slaves were running from slave states to free states as the Constitution was being debated and written.

Delegates whose wealth included slaves did not want their valuable property to pick up, run off, and emancipate themselves in a free state, and insisted that a law be enacted giving them the right to reclaim their runaway property.

This was still the Age of Revolution, and the spirit of freedom still lived in many hearts. A number of Americans were disturbed by the contradiction of recently fighting a war for independence while at the same time living in a nation that upheld slavery.

Some states began gradually to abolish slavery. For example, Pennsylvania enacted a law stating that a slave born after 1780 would be treated as an indentured servant and freed after the age of twenty-eight. The Massachusetts courts abolished slavery in 1783. Connecticut, Rhode Island, New York, and New Jersey all took steps toward gradual emancipation during the years 1784 to 1786.

Gradual Emancipation

In most of the states practicing gradual emancipation, the laws applied mainly to children born after the law had been passed. They would be freed once they attained a certain age. Depending on the state, the age when a person would be freed ranged from eighteen to twenty-eight years old.

By 1784, just one year after the war ended, antislavery societies had sprung up in New York and New Jersey. The Philadelphia antislavery society, first founded in 1775, was revived. In the next six years, people in Delaware, Maryland, Connecticut, and Rhode Island would all establish organizations dedicated to abolishing slavery throughout the nation.

These early antislavery societies included men such as Benjamin Franklin, John Jay, Alexander Hamilton, and Noah Webster. They were important leaders in law, education, and government. As long as slavery was legal, slaves were valuable property—as valuable as a house or a horse. Although members of these societies believed that slavery was immoral, they also felt that helping a slave run away was the same as stealing. These men were property owners themselves. In eighteenth-century America and Europe, a man's position in society was often defined by his wealth and possessions. Some of these early abolitionists felt that slave owners should be compensated for any losses they suffered because of their capital investment in slaves.

Therefore the members of these antislavery societies did not snatch slaves out of the South, although they did help stranded fugitives with food, clothing, and shelter, often with a free black family. In some cases they even found employment for fugitives. They did not conceal fugitives in tunnels in their homes or ride down dark roads at night with runaways hidden in the bottoms of their wagons; these organizations tried to work within the system.

The Pennsylvania Society, the New York Manumission Society, and other anti-slavery organizations worked to have the laws changed. They wrote and distributed pamphlets condemning slavery and petitioned state and local governments. The societies also tried to negotiate with individual slave owners, at times purchasing a slave's freedom themselves.

In 1793, Congress passed the Fugitive Slave Act to strengthen the law that had been written into the Constitution in 1787. The call by slave owners for a stronger law is another indication that slaves were running, because there were more places to run and more free black communities—even in the South—to find refuge in.

It is unfortunate that the Founding Fathers did not abolish slavery once and for all, for it did not die the natural death that some of them thought it would. Maybe some of the delegates thought of slavery as a necessary evil for the

BLACK POPULATION CENSUS OF 1790

State	Slaves	Free
Maine		536
New Hampshire	157	630
Vermont		269
Massachusetts		5,369
Rhode Island	958	3,484
Connecticut	2,648	2,771
New York	21,193	4,682
New Jersey	11,423	2,762
Pennsylvania	3,707	6,531
Delaware	8,887	3,899
Maryland	103,036	8,043
Virginia	292,627	12,866
North Carolina	100,783	5,041
South Carolina	107,094	1,801
Georgia	29,264	398
Kentucky	12,430	114
Tennessee	3,417	361

Source: *Negro Population in the United States, 1790–1915* (New York: Arno Press and the New York Times, 1968), 57.

Free Blacks

Reviewing the laws and ordinances of various states reveals that although "free" blacks were not enslaved, they were not fully free. In some Northern states blacks could not vote and could not sit on juries, and black children could not attend school with white youngsters. There were also economic restrictions placed on free blacks, forbidding them from pursuing certain trades. Despite the discrimination, Northern blacks managed to establish their own churches, schools, and self-help organizations. They also publicly protested their grievances, presenting petitions to various local and state governments.

Free blacks in the South were even more repressed and restricted than their Northern brethren. They had to carry papers showing that they were free, or else they would be declared a fugitive slave. They could not testify in court or sit on a jury. In some Southern states they had to be registered; in others they had to pay a special head tax. For example, in 1756, the South Carolina General Assembly levied a tax on all free African Americans between the ages of twenty-one and fifty years old. If the tax was not paid, the free individual would be sold into slavery.

The threat and reality of being kidnapped and enslaved loomed over both Northern and Southern free African Americans. They were limited in where they lived and where they traveled, sometimes by law and often for safety reasons. Despite restrictions and limitations, the free black populations of both North and South played a significant role in the Underground Railroad movement.

Tag identifying a free black person as a railroad worker

Tag identifying a slave as an overseer

moment. So in a country of free men and women, they chose to retain a class of people who would be defined as property. The people themselves, however, refused to be so defined and continued to try to free themselves.

The passage of the Fugitive Slave Law of 1850 could very well have been the result of this refusal to be defined as property. Between 1830 and 1850 the slavery controversy continued to grow and fester. Notices of slave owners seeking runaways were a common sight in Southern newspapers. Abolitionists, white and black, continued to put increasing pressure on the government; while Southern slave owners continued to demand that the government strengthen the 1793 Fugitive Slave Act, which many people in the free states had been ignoring.

Congress passed the Fugitive Slave Law of 1850 to strengthen the old law of 1793. Some abolitionists said that this new, much harsher law was directed at them; other abolitionists claimed that the new law was so detestable it caused people who had no sympathy for the antislavery movement to become abolitionists.

The new law created commissioners who, along with circuit, county, or district judges, could quickly return an accused fugitive to the person who claimed to own him or her. The enslaved man or woman could offer no testimony in his or her defense. U.S. marshals who refused to arrest a suspected fugitive could be fined a thousand dollars.

The Fugitive Slave Law of 1850 also gave the commissioners and the people appointed by them the authority to gather a posse of citizens to hunt down fugitive slaves. If a citizen refused to help capture a runaway or harbored a runaway, then he or she was breaking the law and could be fined and arrested.

Both the 1793 and the 1850 laws give evidence of the growing intensity of the abolitionist movement as well as the determination of enslaved people to free themselves and gain some control over their lives.

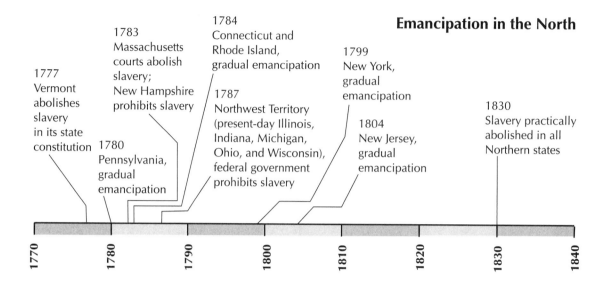

Emancipation in the North

1777 Vermont abolishes slavery in its state constitution

1780 Pennsylvania, gradual emancipation

1783 Massachusetts courts abolish slavery; New Hampshire prohibits slavery

1784 Connecticut and Rhode Island, gradual emancipation

1787 Northwest Territory (present-day Illinois, Indiana, Michigan, Ohio, and Wisconsin), federal government prohibits slavery

1799 New York, gradual emancipation

1804 New Jersey, gradual emancipation

1830 Slavery practically abolished in all Northern states

1770 1780 1790 1800 1810 1820 1830 1840

When John Thompson and a friend escaped slavery in Maryland in the 1830s, they were in constant danger of being returned to slavery under the Fugitive Slave Law:

> We at last reached Columbia, Pennsylvania, where we intended to stop and hire out to work. But the people advised us to go on farther, as already there were two slave hunters in the place in pursuit of two fugitives, whom they had traced to that place. Accordingly we started again the following night, and after travelling about ten miles, reached the house of an elderly Quaker, who offered us a home with him until he could get places for us. These he soon procured, and we went to work; and oh, how sweet the reflection that I was working for myself. We remained here about six months, when we were again routed by the arrival of slave hunters, who had already taken two women and some children, and were in pursuit of other fugitives. In consequence of this, many of the colored people were leaving this for safer parts of the country; so we concluded to go to Philadelphia. I went first, and my friend soon followed. We

had not been there many days, before he was met and recognized by a lady, in Chestnut Street; but he feigned ignorance of her, and did not answer when she addressed him. He came directly and told me of the affair, which at first gave me great alarm, but as we heard nothing more from her, our fears gradually subsided. My friend soon married, and not long after moved to Massachusetts, [after] seeing his old master in one of the streets of Philadelphia, peering into the face of every colored man who happened to pass.

—*from* The Life of John Thompson, a Fugitive Slave, Written by Himself

Chapter 4

Running
The WPA Slave Narratives

In previous chapters, we have looked at evidence for the Underground Railroad in the form of archaeological artifacts found at digs, information listed on shipping registers, and facts and assumptions drawn from reading the law. In this chapter we will consider evidence in the form of the firsthand oral accounts of enslaved men and women themselves.

During the Great Depression of the 1930s the federal government created the Works Progress Administration (WPA), providing jobs for millions of unemployed Americans. One of the most important and lasting WPA projects was the Slave Narrative Collection. It is a compilation of more than two thousand interviews with men and women who had survived slavery and were still living in the South.

Today, the entire collection can be found in the Library of Congress. This oral history gives us a firsthand account of what life was like for enslaved men and women from their point of view. We have the rare privilege of "hearing" their voices as they tell us what they felt and experienced.

Like any other historical document, these narratives must be weighed against various sources, such as official records, newspapers, personal correspondence, and other accounts. The men and women interviewed for the WPA narratives were in their seventies, eighties, and nineties, and were very young children when slavery ended. Some scholars feel that the age of the interviewees does not detract from the validity of the narratives and their use as historical documents. Individuals who are healthy, one scholar pointed out, usually have good mental functions even at advanced ages. People also tend to remember the important moments in their lives: losing a loved one, witnessing a brutal beating, bearing a child, running away.

The WPA narratives differ from the narratives collected by abolitionists and published in pamphlets for propaganda purposes, to show the public the horrors of slavery. Most of those narratives were given by people who had escaped slavery or who had either purchased their own freedom or been freed. The WPA narratives tell the stories of people who remained enslaved until the end of the Civil War.

Some of the WPA narratives are very informative, giving us vivid details and pulling us into the world of the antebellum South. Others are short and

Frederick Douglass (1818–1895)

One of the most famous fugitive slaves, escaping from Maryland in 1838, Douglass became an orator, eloquently speaking out against slavery at abolitionist meetings. He was also a journalist, newspaper editor, and one of the most influential African American nineteenth-century leaders. His classic autobiography, *Narrative of the Life of Frederick Douglass, an American Slave, Written by Himself,* is still in print.

Albumen print by Warren's Portraits, c. 1880s

sketchy, especially when the person interviewed was too young at the time he or she was enslaved to provide reliable and useful information.

The more detailed responses and longer narratives give us a view of slavery from those who endured it. As we continue our search, we can compare several of these narratives with other sources of information—court petitions and ads for runaways—and see how together they provide evidence for an Underground Railroad and its beginnings in the South.

Many of the narrators talk about runaways. Running was a form of rebellion—to abscond with your own body. Comparing the narratives with court records, wanted ads in newspapers, and legal petitions, we see that many slaves fought against their condition and did not accept their fate passively.

Some of the narrators in the collection describe running away and staying only a few weeks. This practice, called "outlying," was one of the few ways to get a break from the endless labor, to obtain something you wanted, or just to express your anger. Delicia Patterson was ninety-two years old when she gave the following interview describing her own experience as a runaway:

I was born in Boonville, Missouri, January 2, 1845. My mother's name was Maria and my father's was Jack Wiley. Mother had five children but raised only two of us. I was owned by Charles Mitchell until I was 15 years old. . . .

I was sold to a Southern Englishman named Thomas B. Steele for $1500. . . . I stayed on with them [Steele and his wife] until one day, while I had a fly brush in my hand fanning flies while they ate, she [Mrs. Steele] told him something I done she didn't like. Just to please her, he taken the fly brush out of my hand and just tapped me with it. It didn't hurt me a bit, but it made me so mad I just went straight to the kitchen, left all the dishes, put on my sunbonnet and run away.

I stayed two weeks. He sent everybody he thought knew where I was after me, and told them to tell me if I would only come on back home, no one

Slave Rebellions

While some people ran away in order to free themselves, others resisted slavery in more violent ways. Slave revolts and attempted revolts occurred throughout North and South America and the Caribbean during many centuries of slavery. In 1791 on the Caribbean island of Haiti, Toussaint L'Ouverture led a successful revolt that freed enslaved men and women from their French masters. On August 30, 1800, nine years after the Haitian revolt, Gabriel Prosser attempted a slave rebellion outside Richmond, Virginia. Someone told authorities about Prosser's plans and he, along with thirty-five of his followers, was hanged.

In 1822, Denmark Vesey, possibly inspired by Toussaint L'Ouverture, tried to carry out a slave revolt in Charleston, South Carolina. His plans were also thwarted, and Vesey and his followers were hanged. Nat Turner's rebellion was carried out in Southampton, Virginia, over three days in August 1831 and ended only after more than fifty whites were killed. Turner escaped from the militia sent out to quell the rebellion and was not captured until October. He was hanged on November 11, 1831.

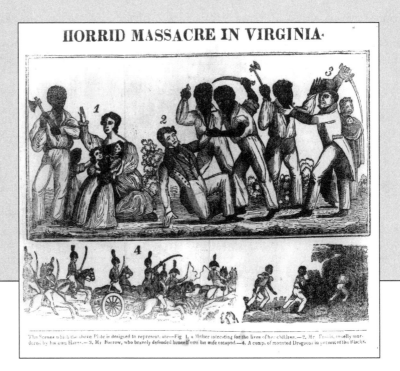

would ever bother me anymore. I hid in the woods that whole two weeks and was not afraid. I would be afraid out in those woods now. . . . At night I would come up to some of the slave cabins who were my friends and eat and stay all night. So I went back home after my 2 weeks off as a runaway . . . and no one ever bothered me any more either.

Not every runaway was treated like Delicia Patterson. Esther Easter, eighty-five years old, describes a beating she witnessed when she was a slave in Missouri:

I done see one whipping and that enough. They wasn't no fooling about it. A runaway slave from the Henkin's plantation was brought back and there was a public whipping, so's the slaves could see what happens when they tries to get away. The runaway was chained to the whipping post, and I was full of misery when I see the lash cutting deep into that boy's skin. He swell up like a dead horse, but he gets over it, only he was never no 'count for work no more.

Julia Brown, who was also eighty-five years old when she was interviewed, had been a slave in Georgia. She too talks about runaways:

Sometimes the slaves would run away. Their masters was mean to them that caused them to run away. Sometimes they would live in caves. They got along all right—what with other people slippin' things into 'em. And, too, they'd steal hogs, chickens and anything else they could get their hands on. Some white people would help, too, for there was some white people who didn't believe in slavery.

Most likely these were whites who lived in the area—not necessarily abolitionists, but Southerners who were against slavery. Anthony Dawson was 105 years old when he was interviewed in Tulsa, Oklahoma, and specifically mentions the Underground Railroad as he talks about his time as a slave in Greenville, North Carolina:

My pappy was the blacksmith. This boy got out in the big road to walk in the soft sand and 'long come a wagon with a white . . . and five, six [blacks] going somewhere. They stopped and told that boy to get in and ride. That was the last anybody seen him. That [white man] and another one was caught after awhile and showed up to be underground railroaders. They would take a bunch of [blacks] into town for some excuse and on the way just pick up a extra [black] and show him where to go to get on the "railroad system." When the runaway . . . got to the North they had to go in the army, and that boy from our place got killed. He was a good boy, but they just talked him into it. Them railroaders was honest, and they didn't take no presents, but the patrollers was low white trash!

Dawson makes another observation similar to Julia Brown's:

They was all kinds of white folks just like they is now. One man . . . would shoot you if you tried to run away. Maybe another . . . would help slip you out to the underground and say "God bless you . . ."

One historian writing about the Underground Railroad says almost the same thing as Anthony Dawson and Julia Brown. He believed that there were individual acts of kindness on the part of some Southerners who would help fugitives with food or directions and not turn them in to the sheriff or the patrollers. He could not verify, however, that there was an Underground Railroad operation running straight from the South to the North.

Silas Jackson, who labored on a Virginia farm, mentions the Underground Railroad and Harriet Tubman:

My father was a man of large stature and my mother was tall and stately. They originally came from the eastern shore of Maryland. . . . The only thing I know about my grandparents were: My grandfather ran away through the aid of Harriet Tubman and went to Philadelphia and saved three hundred and fifty dollars, and purchased my grandmother through the aid of a Quaker or an Episcopal minister, I do not know. I have on several occasions tried to trace this part of my family's past history, but without success.

Petitions filed in county courthouses tell stories similar to the ones told in the slave narratives. Enslaved men and women in South Carolina, for example, often ran to its many swamps, forests, and waterways. On December 9, 1824, white residents and slave owners in several South Carolina counties presented a petition to the South Carolina State Senate that reveals how prevalent runaway camps were in some parts of the state. The petitioners are asking for the freedom of an enslaved man, Royal, because he helped capture a runaway slave named Joe. This long petition, signed by approximately ninety men, reads like a story.

Joe was accused of murdering a white man at Black River near Georgetown, South Carolina, on May 28, 1821. Whether Joe was guilty is unclear. The writers of the petition, possibly exaggerating some of the comments about Joe, state that "he plunged deeper and deeper into crime until neither fear nor danger could deter him first from threatening and then from executing a train of mischiefs [crimes] we believe quite without a parrellel in this country."

The "mischiefs" may have also been some of the same things Julia Brown mentions in her narrative, describing runaway slaves stealing hogs, chickens, and other food. Joe may have been breaking into plantation buildings and stealing articles that he could sell. The petition goes on to say that if Joe were not caught and punished, it would lead to "insubordination and insurrection" among the other slaves.

Joe remained at large for three years. The petition claims that Joe robbed plantations and committed other crimes. He is described as "artful and cunning," the leader of other runaway slaves. But even the offer of generous rewards for information about Joe did not lead to his capture.

Finally, the residents of the area where Joe was hiding organized a militia and went into the swamp to flush out the runaway and his followers. This was war. The petitioners describe how they organized several companies of infantry and "scoured Santee River Swamp."

For two weeks the infantry unsuccessfully searched the swamp, battling heat, humidity, insects, snakes, and animals. By October 6, 1823, exhausted and discouraged, they gave up the search. The slave Royal came to the rescue, however, and offered to help the militia. He led the search party straight to the camp where Joe and other fugitives were hiding.

Somehow Royal talked Joe into coming out of hiding. Maybe he offered help in the way of food or clothing. Meanwhile the militia hid in the flatboat they had used to navigate the swamp and waited for the fugitives to emerge. As the runaways approached the boat, they must have sensed that something was wrong, and they started to run. The militia fired on the fleeing fugitives, but, according to information in the petition, the runaways had muskets, too, and fired back.

In the end, Joe and three men with him were killed. Some of the remaining runaways were sent back to their owners to face severe whippings, while others were executed for attempted murder. For his help in finding Joe and the fugitive camp, Royal was freed. The State of South Carolina paid his owner Royal's purchase price.

Did Royal inform on the runaways so that he would be freed? Were there other cases similar to this one? Perhaps. Slave owners at times used favored and trusted slaves to spy on other slaves. Or was Royal such a loyal slave that he thought it was a crime to run away?

We will never know why Royal informed on the fugitives; his words and thoughts were not recorded. This incident shows us, however, that enslaved people had a world and a life that was hidden from their owners. Robert Smalls, a former slave who made a daring escape during the Civil War, said that masters knew nothing of the "secret life" of their slaves: "One life they show their masters and another life they don't show."

How did Royal know exactly where Joe's camp was? Royal, who appeared to have been a loyal slave, not rebellious and given to running away, knew exactly where to find the runaways' camp. Had he or someone he knew helped fugitives in the past? How many other slaves in the region of the Santee Swamp could have just as easily found Joe's camp?

The legislative records of the South Carolina General Assembly describe another case, this one from 1825, in which a family ran away together. It was somewhat unusual for families to flee because of the difficulty of running and hiding with children, but some families made the attempt.

In Christ Church Parish, South Carolina, a father, mother, and three children left their plantation and headed for nearby woods, where they joined other runaways. They managed to hold onto their stolen freedom for three years. The mother even gave birth to another child.

Their escape must have been well planned. They had to provide their children with food, shelter, and clothing. They had to know where to hide. Most of all, they had to have a network of people—slaves on surrounding plantations and runaways who had already escaped—to help them survive.

But it was a dangerous and furtive existence. They could not simply walk along dark roads at night and slip onto plantations. Their owner or owners (the husband and wife may have belonged to different slaveholders) would have placed notices in the newspapers. A family of runaways would be difficult to disguise. They had to be on the constant lookout for slave catchers and patrollers.

Probably in a raid against their runaway camp similar to the action that flushed out Joe in the Santee Swamp, the family was caught. The parents were killed, and the children "surrendered" and returned to slavery.

Often one reason for taking a chance and running with children was the threat of being sold away from a mate or a child. Sometimes, though, enslaved men and women ran because they knew that punishment for a crime or an affront to a master or mistress would be swift and brutal.

Leah Garrett of Richmond County, Georgia, tells the story of another family hiding together. Their story, however, had a happier ending:

I know so many things 'bout slavery time 'til I never will be able to tell 'em all. . . . One of the slaves married a young gal, and they put her in the "Big House" to work. One day Mistress jumped on her 'bout something and the gal hit her back. Mistress said she was goin' to have Marster put her in the stock and beat her when he come home. When the gal went to the field and told her husband 'bout it, he told her where to go and stay till he got there.

That night he took his supper to her. He carried her to a cave and hauled pine straw and put in there for her to sleep on. . . . He fixed that cave up just like a house for her, put a stove in there and run the pipe out through the ground into a swamp. Everybody always wondered how he fixed that pipe, course they didn't cook on it 'til night when nobody could see the smoke.

He ceiled the house with pine logs, made beds and tables out of pine poles, and they lived in this cave seven years. Durin' this time they had three children. . . . The seven years she lived in the cave, different folks helped them in food.

Her husband would take it to a certain place and she would go and get it. People had passed over this cave ever so many times, but nobody knowed these folks was livin' there. Our Marster didn't know whar she wuz.

This family hid in plain sight. At first the narrative might seem far-fetched, but Julia Brown in her narrative also talks about people hiding in caves. There were enslaved men, like the husband in this story, who knew how to survive under arduous conditions. These were people who were used to a hard, rugged life.

Ishrael Massie, who had been a slave in Virginia, tells a similar story about his half-brother, who ran away and hid in the woods:

He had a vault in the woods fixed just like this room and he had a wife and two boys that he raised under there. . . . There was a hole cut in the ground. I . . . cut a many a one and stole lumber at night to cover it over with. Then dirt was piled on top of this plank so that it won't rain in there. Then he has him some piping—trough-like—made of wood that runned so many feet in the ground. This carried smoke way away from this cave. . . . [They] used oak bark 'cause it didn't give much smoke. He had him a hole to come up on land. There was sticks, pine beard, and trash on top to cover the hole. . . . You could stand right over this hole and wouldn't know it.

This cave was not far from the creek. Reasons for that is you could get water . . . all us slaves knew where he was but, in them days you know . . . didn't tell on each other. Yes, yes I . . . ate many a good meal . . . in Bob's den.

Why did some runaways stay in the same vicinity? Why didn't they try to escape to Ohio or Pennsylvania or any of the free states that had opened up after the Revolutionary War? Why didn't they run to Canada where they would not be subject to the Fugitive Slave Law of 1793?

One of the main reasons for staying close to familiar territory was attachment to family and friends. For some, emotional ties to loved ones were even stronger than the bonds of slavery. Also, staying close to "home" meant staying close to help. Most fugitives had relatives and acquaintances on nearby plantations and farms.

There was another, practical reason for staying in familiar territory: unless the runaways had traveled with their owners or had been hired out to work in another town or county, most of them were not familiar with the geography of the surrounding area. The movements of the majority of enslaved men or women were confined to the plantations and farms where they had always lived and worked. How could they make the trip from South Carolina or Alabama to Canada unless they had help?

Lizzie Williams speaks in her narrative about the problem of not knowing where to run. She had been a slave in Alabama:

Lots of the poor [blacks] run away, but weren't no use. There weren't no place to go. They was always lookin' for you and then you had to work harder than ever, besides all kinds of punishment you got . . .

On the other hand, some fugitives ran far away from the plantations and farms where they lived. As Southern cities and towns grew during the nineteenth century, new roads to freedom opened up to those attempting to emancipate themselves.

One of the narratives talks of slaves escaping across the Rio Grande into Mexico. Jacob Branch, who had been a slave in Texas, explains that "in this part [slaves] heads for the Rio Grande River. The Mexicans rig up flatboats out in the middle [of] the river, tied to stakes with rope. When the colored people gets to the rope they can pull theyself 'cross the rest of the way on them boats.

The white folks rode the American side [of] that river all the time, but plenty slaves get through, anyway."

For a number of fugitives, their destination was not a free state in the North, but a Southern city with a free black population that they could blend into and obtain help from. In the Deep South, thousands of runaways found the roads and waterways that led to cities like Charleston and New Orleans. In many cases, slaves who ran to these cities knew free people of color who could help them. Fugitives who could read had a better chance of passing successfully as free persons, and if they were skilled workers, they might remain free for years.

A petition to the South Carolina House of Representatives that was signed by a group of citizens in 1829 complains about the increase in the number of runaways from Christ Church Parish because of its proximity to the city of Charleston. The petitioners complain that "their parish being surrounded by navigable water leading directly to, and occasioning much intercourse with the City, and from the great Northern road passing through their parish in its whole length [the petitioners] are . . . exposed to the great evil of absconding slaves."

The petition also touches on why slaves are running: "Changes in the prices of our crops and . . . in the fortunes of many of our fellow Citizens, have taken place and these changes have carried to Charleston for sale, large bodies of Negroes. The unrestrained [communication] of these with free blacks and low and worthless white people during their sojourn there, has infused into the minds of the [N]egroes ideas of insubordination and of emancipation which they carry with them when sold into every part of the State."

This petition is evidence that the threat as well as the reality of being sold away causes people to run. It also shows the slave owners' dislike of free blacks, seen as a danger to the slave system—people who would give slaves ideas about living free as well.

We do not know who the "low and worthless" whites were. Were they simply poor whites? Were they runaway indentured servants, or criminals who had escaped and were living as outlaws? Or were they Southerners with antislavery sentiments? Or whites from the North and West? The petition doesn't say, but there seems to be so much anger in the words that perhaps they were people who were against slavery—which would make them even more hated than criminals. The petition does mention the "increasing efforts made by enthusiasts out of Carolina, to poison the minds of our domestic people." This clearly seems to be a reference to abolitionists.

In rural areas a stranger stood out, and a black stranger would be stopped by patrollers and arrested or beaten if he or she did not have a pass. Many of the narratives mention patrollers. Daniel Dowdy talks about them in his narrative: "Oh, them patrollers! They had a chief and he get 'em together and if they caught you without a pass and sometimes with a pass, they'd beat you."

It was more difficult to control slaves in the city because, in addition to free people of color, there were also slaves who had been hired out, and sometimes a slave owner would allow a slave to hire himself or herself out. In other words, enslaved men or women would find work and pay their owners a portion of the money they earned. This was considered illegal by local authorities but was done anyway. Smart runaways who reached the cities could often find work by claiming that they had permission from their owners to hire themselves out.

A merchant who needed a strong young man to haul barrels, or an elderly widow who wanted a housekeeper, or a blacksmith who wanted an assistant to shoe horses, or a ship captain who was short on experienced hands might not inspect freedom papers carefully or might readily believe that the person looking for work was a slave hiring himself or herself out.

Just as many of the runaways fleeing to swamps and forests were eventually caught and punished, some slaves who escaped to regions far from where they

Property for Sale

Notices such as the following are evidence that people were treated as property and sold along with horses, mules, and wagons. A sale, as described in the notice below, was often the motive for running away.

LARGE SALE OF REAL AND PERSONAL PROPERTY—ESTATE SALE.

On Monday, the (7th) seventh day of February next, I will sell at Auction, without reserve, at the Plantation, near Linden, all the Horses, Mules, Wagons, Farming Utensils, Corn, Fodder, &c. And on the following Monday (14th), the fourteenth day of February next, at the Court House, at Linden, in Marengo County, Alabama, I will sell at public auction, without reserve, to the highest bidder, 110 PRIME AND LIKELY NEGROES, belonging to the estate of the late John Robinson of South Carolina. Among the Negroes are four valuable Carpenters, and a very superior Blacksmith.

lived in bondage were also eventually caught. A talented young slave was a source of income. The loss of slave property was as traumatic to a slave owner as the loss of land, or a home, or some other valuable possession.

Slave owners did not shrug their shoulders and move on to other matters when a slave ran away. It was considered serious business. Notices for runaways were a common sight in many Southern papers. Notices were also posted in towns and counties surrounding the place the fugitive had fled.

Besides sending out slave catchers and hound dogs, owners contacted the runaway's relatives and known acquaintances on other plantations. Those who could afford to do so even hired agents who would travel to other states to hunt down a fugitive.

A number of runaways were eventually caught and returned to the plantations and farms where they had labored. Some were seized after a few weeks; others remained free for years before being caught by a relentless master or mistress who had never given up the search.

Who took the chance to run? Runaway notices, petitions, and other court records show that men and women, old and young, whole families, single parents with children, and even children alone all ran away. The largest and most successful group of runaways, however, were young men in their twenties. They had the strength and stamina to deal with the hardships of life as a fugitive. Also, most younger men were single and childless, so there were fewer emotional ties.

The reasons for running were varied—an abusive owner, an accusation of committing a crime, or the actual commission of a crime. The main reason for taking to the road, however, was to find or be with a loved one—a husband, wife, mother, father, or child who had been sold away.

When a slaveholder died and the assets of the estate had to be sold, the enslaved men, women, and children did not know what would happen to them, except that they would be sold away to serve new masters. Whenever an estate was sold, enslaved families faced separation—human emotions were not considered when property was being auctioned off to the highest bidder. If a slave owner was bankrupt and had to sell his or her property, enslaved men, women, and children were sold along with the house, land, and other property. These disruptions and separations necessarily took an emotional toll on the slaves. Rather than leave their fate in the hands of people who saw them as property only, some slaves attempted to take control of their lives and ran.

These fugitives in the South, especially in the years after the Revolution, were the forerunners of the Underground Railroad movement. They operated in secret and had help from others in the form of food, clothing, shelter, hiding places, and travel directions. They knew how to avoid slave catchers and dogs trained specifically to hunt them down.

Ishrael Massie still remembered after so many years: "If you are running away, jump in the creek. Dogs lose the scent of you and too, if you take a raw onion [and] rub feet bottom you make the dogs lose you."

Slaves knew the roads that led to swamps and forests, cities and towns. How did they find the strength and spirit to keep going?

Chapter 5

Steal Away
The Enslaved Speak through Spirituals

When we think about following the Underground Railroad through the physical evidence that remains, we often think in terms of learning facts: names, dates, places, how many ran away, what people wore, what they ate. But can we ever know how they felt? Perhaps by examining the texts of slave spirituals, we can begin to hear evidence of the emotions that went with being enslaved.

Can we put ourselves in the shoes of an enslaved person? Can we really imagine how children must have felt when they were separated from their parents, or how husbands and wives felt when they were sold away from each other? And can we actually know how it must feel to have no control over any aspect of your life? You cannot take a walk down the road when you feel like it. You can't change jobs if you don't like the one you have. Learning how to read and write is illegal for you and can bring great punishment.

You might not even be able to choose your mate, because he or she lives on another plantation. Or you might be forced to mate with someone you do not want to be with: your owner thinks that because you are a strong and healthy girl or guy, your partner should be, too, so that your children will be healthy and strong—a sound investment.

And even though you might be owned by someone who is not cruel, who feeds you and clothes you decently and even gives you some privileges, you are still a slave. You have no rights, no equality under the law, and no justice if you are wronged.

Where, then, do you find the strength and spirit to meet each new day, and how do you find the courage to defy a system that seems so much more powerful than you are? Enslaved Africans might have lost every material possession when they were brought across the Atlantic to a life of slavery, but they did not lose their humanity. An important part of that humanity was their great oral traditions. For the millions of Africans caught in slavery's web, their ability to transfer a variety of cultural traditions to their new setting helped them survive the horror and degradation of bondage.

Enslaved Africans came from different cultures and spoke different languages. Their common language was music. Those rhythms and harmonies, along with the musical tradition of call and response — one person leads the song and a chorus responds to the leader—became the foundation of the music enslaved Africans would create in America, music with roots deep in Africa, which has profoundly influenced American music.

Music was and is a powerful element in traditional West African culture. Music and dance were not merely reserved for social events, but touched almost every aspect of people's lives—from birth to death. Not only were religious beliefs communicated through music and dance, but poetry, drama, stories, and social commentary were all expressed in music and song. In West Africa, "talking" drums were one way to communicate. Slave owners in America knew the power of the music and forbade drumming.

Although we have the written and oral narratives that give us some idea of who these enslaved people were, what they thought, how they felt, from their perspective, some scholars believe that the body of music we call "spirituals" could very well be a window into the hearts and souls of enslaved men and women in America. Through spirituals people held in bondage expressed directly, and not through someone else's interpretation, their deepest feelings about their lives and the difficult world they lived in.

The scholar and writer W. E. B. Du Bois, whose grandfather was born into slavery, wrote in 1903 that although some spirituals reflected a people who could be full of joy, most were "the music of an unhappy people, of the children of disappointment; they tell of death and suffering and unvoiced longing toward a truer world, of misty wanderings and hidden ways."

Spirituals tell us about the slaves' struggle to survive; they express a longing for justice; and they talk about finding a way to freedom.

Another scholar and theologian made

Quilts

Just as enslaved Africans carried their oral traditions from Africa to the Americas, they also brought with them other expressions of their culture. Researchers and scholars analyzing the function of decorative and folk art in African American history and culture suggest that quilting patterns similar to textile designs used in various West African cultures were handed down from generation to generation among African Americans. Some researchers believe that quilting patterns used by enslaved Africans in America may have also functioned as coded messages helping runaways in their flight to freedom. A quilt with a particular pattern, hanging outside a window or across a porch railing to air, might indicate a specific direction that a traveler should follow. There remains much interesting research to be done in this area.

a similar statement: "Simply put, what Black people are singing religiously will provide a clue as to what is happening to them sociologically."

Spirituals were not only songs of sorrow and hope, but may have contained hidden messages. Is the well-known spiritual "Go Down, Moses" only about the flight of the Hebrews from Egypt as told in the Bible? Or is it really about the plight of enslaved people in America? Is "ole Pharaoh" the slave master and "Israel" enslaved Africans?

Go Down, Moses,

Way down in Egypt land.

Tell ole Pharaoh

To let my people go.

Go down, Moses,

Way down in Egypt land.

Tell ole Pharaoh

To let my people go.

When Israel was in Egypt land,

Let my people go,

Oppressed so hard they could not stand,

Let my people go.

When spoke the Lord, bold Moses said,

Let my people go.

If not I'll smite your first-born dead,

Let my people go.

To the ears of the slave owner this might have been just a simplistic inter-pretation of the story of Exodus in the Old Testament that slaves had heard a preacher tell. But masks, symbols, and the use of double meanings were very much a part of West African rituals. The same devices could be employed in the music African American slaves created. Enslaved people were used to hiding their true selves from those who owned them.

"Go Down, Moses" undoubtedly expressed the slaves' desire for their own Moses, someone who would bring their Pharaoh to his knees and free them. The spirituals created centuries ago by enslaved Africans in America were not only expressions of religious ideas but appear also to have doubled as coded messages aiding escaping slaves. These songs are still sung in many African American churches today.

It is not possible to give exact dates for the creation of these spirituals, since so many of them were sung in secret. We do know, however, that in 1740 a period of religious fervor called the Great Awakening spread through the colonies. Black and white itinerant preachers visited plantations and farms, and a number of slaves were converted to Christianity. Some of the black preachers were also slaves, but were allowed to preach on a few plantations and farms in their neighborhoods. It is possible that spirituals were first heard in the mid- to late 1760s. Five to six hundred of these songs have been preserved.

Some slave masters would not allow their human property to congregate for any reason, and on their plantations, only white preachers were allowed to give religious instruction. Or, if the slaves conducted their own worship services, then a member of the slaveholder's family or some other white person had to be there to keep an eye and an ear on the master's property. On some plantations slaves were required to attend the same church as their owners but were segregated from the white worshipers. On other plantations they received no religious instruction at all. Despite spotty and distorted religious exposure, enslaved men and women over a period of time took the stories of the Old Testament and the principles of Christianity and interpreted in their own way this religion that had been imposed on them.

In his WPA narrative, Richard Carruthers describes the kind of religious instruction he received on the plantation in Texas where he had been enslaved: "When the white preacher come he preach and pick up his Bible and claim he gettin' the text right out from the Good Book and he preach: 'The Lord say, don't you steal chickens from your missus. Don't you steal your master's hogs.' That would be all he preach."

Carruthers explains how he and the other slaves would go out into the fields about midnight, away from the eyes and ears of the master: "[We] used to have a prayin' ground down in the hollow and sometime we come out of the field, between eleven and twelve at night, scorchin' and burnin' up with nothin' to eat, and we wants to ask the good Lord to have mercy."

The African Methodist Episcopal Church

Black churches, some beginning in bush arbors on Southern plantations, are among the most enduring and strongest of African American institutions. In 1787 Richard Allen, who had purchased his freedom from a Delaware farmer, founded the Free African Society, a benevolent organization. When Allen and other black worshipers at a white Philadelphia church were segregated during services, he and members of the Free African Society established the Mother Bethel A.M.E. (African Methodist Episcopal) Church. By 1816, A.M.E. churches had grown in number, becoming the first black Christian religious denomination. These congregations worked closely with Quakers and other abolitionists. It is said that escaped slaves were hidden in the basement of Mother Bethel A.M.E. Church in Philadelphia. Some slaves escaping from the South and reaching Philadelphia and other Northern cities would surely have brought with them the spirituals that guided and sustained them in their journey.

Richard Allen, center, and other bishops of the African Methodist Episcopal Church, the first African American religious denomination. Lithograph, c. 1876.

It was in these secret meetings away from masters and overseers that enslaved men and women created the spirituals we still sing today. Indeed, the song most connected with the American civil rights movement is "We Shall Overcome," which comes from the spiritual "I Shall Overcome Someday."

Richard Carruthers does not give a detailed description of the slaves' worship services, but from other accounts as well as information gathered by scholars and researchers, we can imagine how a spiritual would be created in the dark of night in a secret "prayer ground."

Perhaps Carruthers or someone else at the service calls out, "Nobody knows the trouble I see, Lord." Another person responds, "Nobody knows like Jesus." And the rest of the worshipers begin to add to the words. Perhaps the first person who called out, "Nobody knows the trouble I see," sings it this time with a distinct melody. Maybe someone at that meeting is sent to another plantation and participates in another worship service and remembers the song. He or she calls out, "Nobody knows the trouble I see." And so a spiritual is born and catches on, as it is repeated with variations from plantation to plantation and farm to farm and is even carried to the cities of the North:

> Nobody knows the trouble I see, Lord,
> Nobody knows the trouble I see,
> Nobody knows like Jesus.
> Brothers will you pray for me,
> Brothers will you pray for me,
> Brothers will you pray for me,
> An' help me to drive ole Satan away.

Perhaps in this spiritual "Satan" refers not only to the devil but to the slave master as well.

Although Richard Carruthers does not talk about specific spirituals, he does explain how he used a song to send a message to his fellow slaves. Acting as a lookout, he kept an eye on the cotton fields where people were working: "Sometime they lazy 'round and if I see the overseer comin' from the Big House I sings a song to warn 'em, so they not get whipped, and it go like this:

> "Hold up, hold up, American Spirit!
> "Hold up, hold up."

This is clear evidence of the use of a song that has a double meaning and more than one purpose. The words signaled the workers to look busy.

Mary Ella Grandberry, born in slavery in Alabama, was ninety years old when she was interviewed in the 1930s. She recalled that she and the other slaves could not talk about the free states or they would be whipped: "There weren't but one church on the place what I lived on and the colored and the white both went to it. You know we was never allowed to go to church [without] some of the white folks with us. We weren't even allowed to talk with nobody from another farm." Her owner, Mary Ella Grandberry explained, was afraid that they would band together and try to make a run for the North. She also said that the spiritual "Steal Away" was a popular song and that everyone knew it:

> Steal away, steal away,
> Steal away to Jesus!
> Steal away, steal away home,
> I ain't got long to stay here.
> My Lord, He calls me,
> He calls me by the thunder,
> The trumpet sounds within-a my soul,
> I ain't got long to stay here.

It is said that Harriet Tubman, one of the most famous runaways and Underground Railroad workers, sang the spirituals "Steal Away" and "Go Down, Moses" as a signal for other fugitives to meet her at a designated place so that she could lead them to the North. Tubman has been called "the Moses of her people."

Nat Turner may have used the spiritual "Steal Away" to communicate with his followers during his slave revolt in Southampton County, Virginia, and perhaps Denmark Vesey was inspired by the spiritual "Go Down, Moses" during his planned slave revolt in Charleston.

Another spiritual that could possibly have a double meaning is:

Let us break bread together on our knees, yes, on our knees;
Let us break bread together on our knees, yes, on our knees;
When I fall on my knees, with my face to the rising sun,
Oh, Lord, have mercy on me.

This is a familiar spiritual often sung on Communion Sundays. Although it is a call to worship, it may also have been a signal to meet. The words "with my face to the rising sun" might have also contained a hidden message giving directions: to travel eastward.

A song that actually gives directions is "Follow the Drinking Gourd":

Follow the drinking gourd
Follow the drinking gourd.
For the old man is a-waiting for to carry you to freedom,
If you follow the drinking gourd.
When the sun comes back and the first quail calls,
Follow the drinking gourd.
The riverbank would make a mighty good road

Dead trees will show you the way

Left foot, peg foot traveling on

Follow the drinking gourd.

The river ends between two hills

Follow the drinking gourd

There's another river on the other side

Follow the drinking gourd.

The "drinking gourd" refers to the stars in the Big Dipper, guiding travelers to the north.

The following song speaks of auctions, whippings, and slave owners who never stop demanding. It remembers, too, the many thousands who have gone before. It was probably sung in secret, not for the ears of the master or the overseer:

No more auction block for me,

no more, no more.

No more auction block for me,

many thousand go.

No more peck of corn for me,

many thousand go.

No more driver's lash for me,

no more, no more.

No more mistress' call for me,

no more, no more.

No more mistress' call for me,

many thousand go.

The song also expresses hope and deliverance. God would deliver the slaves as He had delivered the Hebrews of the Old Testament:

Didn't my Lord deliver Daniel,
Deliver Daniel, deliver Daniel,
Didn't my Lord deliver Daniel,
An' why not every man?
He delivered Daniel from the lions' den,
Jonah from the belly of the whale,
An' the Hebrew children from the fiery furnace,
An' why not every man?

Frederick Douglass, another famous runaway and abolitionist, said that when he and other men and women in bondage sang the words of the spiritual "O Canaan, sweet Canaan, I am bound for the land of Canaan," it meant "more than a hope of reaching heaven. We meant to reach the north—and the north was our Canaan."

I thought I heard them say,
There were lions in the way,
I don't expect to stay
Much longer here.
Run to Jesus—shun the danger—
I don't expect to stay
Much longer here.

Frederick Douglass said that this was another favorite song with a double meaning: "In the lips of some, it meant the expectation of a speedy summons to a world of spirits; but in the lips of our company, it simply meant a speedy pilgrimage toward a free state, and deliverance from all the evils and dangers of slavery."

Booker T. Washington, who was born into slavery and later became an educator and president of Tuskegee Institute, says almost the same thing in his autobiography, *Up from Slavery*: "Most of the verses of the plantation songs had some reference to freedom. True, they had sung those same verses before, but they had been careful to explain that the 'freedom' in these songs referred to the next world, and had no connection with life in this world. Now they gradually threw off the mask, and were not afraid to let it be known that the 'freedom' in their songs meant freedom . . . in this world."

Thomas Wentworth Higginson, a white abolitionist and officer of the first black regiment of the Civil War, was told by a drummer boy that when slaves sang "The Lord will call us home" in the song "We'll Soon Be Free," "the Lord" really meant the Yankees:

> We'll soon be free,
> We'll soon be free,
> We'll soon be free,
> When the Lord will call us home. . . .
> My brother, how long,
> 'Fore we done sufferin' here?
> It won't be long
> 'Fore the Lord will call us home. . . .

By the 1830s and 1840s the abolitionist movement had grown, and so had the tensions between the free and slave states. The runaway population had also expanded. There were more freedom zones now, and among those fugitives who reached the North, many of them surely sang:

> Oh, freedom!
> Oh, freedom!
> Oh, freedom over me!
> And before I'd be a slave,

I'll be buried in my grave,

And go home to my Lord and be free!

Vinnie Brunson, in her WPA interview, eloquently and simply described the meaning of the spirituals to those who were enslaved:

The slave used to sing to nearly everything he did. It was the way he expressed his feelin's an it made him relieved, if he was happy, it made him happy, if he was sad, it made him feel better, an so he does naturally sings his feelin's. The timber [slave] sings as he cuts the logs and keeps the time with his axe. The women sing as they bend over the washtub, the cotton chopper sing as he chops the cotton. The mother sing as she rocks her baby to sleep. The cotton picker sing as he picks the cotton, an' they all sing in the meetin's an' at the baptizin' and at the funerals. It is the [slave's] mos' joy, an his mos' comfort when he needs all these things. They sing 'bout the joys in the next world an the trouble in this. They first jes sung the religious songs, then they commenced to sing 'bout the life here an when they sang of both they called them the "Spirituals." The old way to sing them was to keep time with the clappin' of the hands an' pattin' of the feet. They sing them in different ways for different occasions, at a meetin' when they shouts they sing it joyful, and when they sing the same song at a funeral they sing it slow an' moanful, when they sing the same song in the fields it is sung, if they work fast, quick, if they is tired it is sung slow. If it is sung at Christmas, then it is sung gay and happy. The days of slavery made the [slave] live his life over in the "spirituals," most of the real old time slaves are gone, jes a few maybe who were boys then, but their song lives on with both the white an' the black folks, we forgets the sorrows . . .

Chapter 6

"I Will Be Heard"
Archaeology Meets an Oral Tradition

Catherine and Carol Lott, both descendants of a Dutch family that settled in Brooklyn, New York, in the 1600s, told the same family story to archaeologists who had been doing research on the family's nineteenth-century farmhouse. They were members of an extended family, but did not know each other. The archaeologists had interviewed each one separately in 1998 and 1999. Both women had been told that in the 1840s slaves were hidden in a second-floor bedroom of the farmhouse. The house, they claimed, was part of the Underground Railroad.

How accurate is this family oral history? Are there any other clues to support the claim that this Brooklyn home was a stop on the Underground Railroad? Is the story merely family legend and myth passed down from generation to generation? Perhaps a family member had seen a program on television about the Underground Railroad and assumed that because the house was pre–Civil War, it was connected to the series of hiding places for fugitive slaves.

The Lott house today

Sometimes historians can use anecdotes, rumors, and handed-down tales as another kind of evidence in their search for the truth about the Underground Railroad. Rather than take them at face value, however, they are careful to see whether other kinds of evidence lend support.

The archaeologists at the Lott house felt that there might be some truth to this legend, based on several facts. Like other Dutch farm families, the Lotts used enslaved Africans as farmworkers and house servants. Farms in New York did not employ slave labor as extensively as Southern farms and plantations. The Lott family owned twelve men and women who lived on the property. The family freed their slaves in 1800, twenty-seven years before slavery was completely abolished in New York State.

Another indication that the family might have been willing to help runaways is that they belonged to the Flatlands Reformed Dutch Church, which, like the Quakers, believed that all people had the right to be free. Hendrick Lott was not only following his church's directives, but perhaps was also endorsing the antislavery movement.

Census records show that the former slaves remained on the property as paid laborers up until about 1840. Evidently, there was a mutual regard between the family and their freed servants and laborers. It is also possible that the Lott servants themselves were hiding fugitive slaves.

The geography of the farm, with small inlets and waterways nearby, would have made an "underground" route by water possible. A runaway fleeing through New Jersey could have crossed one of the waterways going around Staten Island and then headed into Brooklyn. This would have been a safe route to bypass the slave catchers and bounty hunters in Manhattan. (Frederick Douglass tells in his narrative how frightened he was when he first arrived in Manhattan and was warned to beware of slave catchers and kidnappers.)

I SELL THE SHADOW TO SUPPORT THE SUBSTANCE.
SOJOURNER TRUTH.

Sojourner Truth (photographer unknown), 1864. Truth, originally named Isabella, was freed in 1827 when New York State abolished slavery. A very religious woman and charismatic speaker, she traveled extensively and worked tirelessly for the abolitionist cause and the women's rights movement.

The Lott property would have been a perfect hiding place for a fugitive. As we have seen, runaways gravitated to areas where there were free blacks. The farm had enough black people there to help a fugitive. Since the Lott family also had antislavery sentiments, they probably would not have objected to their servants helping and hiding a relative or a friend.

Even before they began to dig, all of this information gave the archaeologists good reason to believe that the Lott house could well have once hidden fugitive slaves. Soon, however, they would have even more compelling evidence in support of the theory.

In 1998, New York City purchased the Lott property, one of the last remaining Dutch-style farmhouses left standing in southern Brooklyn. Nowadays the dilapidated wooden structure sits on less than an acre of land. The nineteenth-century home looks out of place on present-day East 36th Street in the Marine Park section. Cars, buses, and children riding their bicycles pass small, brick two-story houses. It strains our imaginations to picture how the Lott house and this neighborhood once looked—cows grazing on salt-marsh grasses; wheat fields, cornfields, and vegetable gardens; flocks of birds flying over the two-hundred-acre farm. The only remnant of this past is the farmhouse.

The twenty-room home was once the property of Hendrick Lott and his family, Dutch settlers who first came to Brooklyn in 1654. Direct descendants of Hendrick Lott lived in the house until 1989. The Lott home is a historic New York City landmark and is being restored to its original state, described by one nineteenth-century historian as one of the "grandest homes in all of Kings County."

It is here at this farmhouse on the Lott property that the archaeologists began to dig up the past, where they found nineteenth-century ceramic shards and pathways made out of shells. They examined the original structure, built in 1719—a "two-story salt-box style" with an attached lean-to. Excavating, they found evidence that two upstairs rooms may have been living quarters for the servants.

They found artifacts—a pelvis bone from either a sheep or a goat, a cloth pouch tied with hemp, and needles and glass beads. Five dried corncobs were arranged in a geometrical design, suggesting a possible African ritual. As we saw at the Fort Mose site and as we heard in the spirituals, African roots were not entirely severed.

When the investigators studied the portion of the house that was built in the 1800s, they made another discovery. In an upstairs bedroom they found a closet hidden behind wallpaper and newsprint. The hinged back wall of the closet opened to reveal a small passageway that would allow people to hide within the eaves of the house. A coat hook hung above the opening to the passageway. We can imagine this dimly lit closet, in the 1830s, with clothing hiding the door to the passage.

The closet at the Lott house

In considering the possibility that the Lott house harbored runaway slaves, we have looked at reasons why the Lott family might do so and reasons why that particular house was well suited for the purpose. We have noted physical evidence in the form of a secret room, which held artifacts that might have belonged to Africans. We should also think about what was happening at that time in the surrounding area. It's possible that there was a network of safe houses that existed in the boroughs of Brooklyn and Queens in the 1830s and 1840s and that the Lott house was part of it.

Memoirs and family oral histories from nearby Flushing and Long Island tell other stories about helping runaways. A woman by the name of Hannah Jackson, born into one of Flushing's Quaker families, recalled that when she was a child she was not allowed to play in the woods near Flushing Creek on the family farm because her parents did not want her to accidentally reveal the hiding places of runaways the family was helping.

Because there was a large free African American community on Long Island, especially in Westbury, slaves often escaped there. One oral history tells of a fugitive who had been working for Valentine Hicks, a Quaker, being chased down the road by slave catchers. Hicks saw the man running and let him into his home. Hicks had a secret room in his attic for hiding valuables. A closet door two feet off the floor was disguised as a cupboard. Stairs leading up to the attic were hidden behind the door. That night, the man, hidden in a wagon, was taken to Long Island Sound, where he boarded a boat to Westchester County.

Another free black Long Island community could be found in the village of Hempstead, in an area called Jerusalem, founded in 1687 on two hundred acres of land by John Jackson, also a Quaker. The Jackson family freed their slaves after the Revolutionary War, and many of those men and women chose to stay there and work. This community came to be known as "the Brush" because of its thick growth of oak and pine trees. Some of the freedmen received property from their former owners and became farmers themselves. The Brush grew into a thriving community of free blacks and Quakers, as well as a refuge for runaway slaves.

By the 1830s, free black communities like the Brush on Long Island were growing in the North and influencing the antislavery movement. The number of runaways was increasing, and no doubt the Brush would have been a stop on the Underground Railroad. More and more havens for runaways, like the Lott house, were needed as America expanded westward and the slavery issue grew along with it.

Fugitives in the border states—Kentucky, Missouri, Virginia, Maryland, and Delaware—took advantage of their proximity to free states and free black communities. Two of the most famous runaways, Frederick Douglass and Harriet Tubman, both escaped from Maryland.

With an increase in antislavery activity in the free states in the North and the growth of the free black population, it seemed as though by the end of the 1820s the issue of slavery would remain in the public eye and on the public conscience:

I count my life not dear unto me, but I am ready to be offered at any moment. For what is the use of living, when in fact I am dead? But remember, Americans, that as miserable, wretched, degraded and abject as you have made us in the preceding, and in this generation, to support you and your families, some of you [whites], on the continent of America, will yet curse the day that you ever were born. You want slaves, and want us for your slaves!!! My colour will yet root some of you out of the very face of the earth!!!!!

These were only a few of the powerful statements and challenging words that David Walker, a free black abolitionist living in Boston, made in his antislavery pamphlet, *Walker's Appeal, in Four Articles; together with a Preamble, to the Coloured Citizens of the World, but in Particular and Very Expressly to Those of the United States of America,* published in 1829. The title is long, and so was the reach of the publication. The governors of Virginia and North Carolina informed their state legislatures about Walker's publication, and the governor of Georgia asked the mayor of Boston to try to keep the pamphlet out of circulation. David Walker spoke through his pen, proving that the pen was at least as mighty as the sword: "My motive in writing . . . is . . . to awaken in the breasts of my afflicted, degraded and slumbering brethren, a spirit of inquiry and investigation respecting our miseries and wretchedness in this Republican Land of Liberty!!!!!"

No black person in America had ever written anything so controversial or spoken so blatantly. Some people say that Walker's incendiary rhetoric may have fired up Nat Turner.

John Russwurm published *Walker's Appeal* in *Freedom's Journal*, which he had founded in 1827 in New York City. (David Walker sold subscriptions for the paper.) Perhaps the radical white abolitionist John Brown also read *Walker's Appeal*, spurring him on at some point to take violent and direct action in his efforts to eradicate slavery.

No doubt William Lloyd Garrison, who began publishing his famous abolitionist paper, the *Liberator*, in 1831 in Boston, had also read it. And maybe *Walker's Appeal* gave Garrison some ideas about the direction and the effectiveness of the antislavery movement in America.

In 1833 William Lloyd Garrison and other abolitionists organized the American Anti-Slavery Society. Although he angered some members when he insisted on including women and blacks, Garrison recognized that black people had been actively involved in aiding fugitives. While the antislavery movement was trying to end slavery, blacks were focusing on either freeing themselves or helping others to gain their freedom.

Garrison realized that blacks working together with antislavery whites would strengthen the movement. In an article in his newspaper, the *Liberator*, he wrote that he understood how free blacks were "struggling against wind and tide." He could have been alluding to the fact that people in free black communities were

Henry Highland Garnet

Bounty hunters almost recaptured the family of noted abolitionist Henry Highland Garnet two years after they had escaped from Maryland to Manhattan in 1825. The family took refuge in various homes on Long Island. Garnet, greatly influenced by *Walker's Appeal*, gave a speech in Buffalo, New York, in 1843 at the National Convention of Colored Citizens that caused quite a stir. In "An Address to the Slaves of the United States of America," Garnet urged slaves to take matters into their own hands and fight against enslavement even if it meant using violence.

working hard to free enslaved people, some of whom were relatives and friends. Garrison fought against sexism and brought women into the movement as well. He and his followers fashioned a more radical form of antislavery work than his predecessors. They wrote pamphlets and broadsides denouncing slavery. Their meetings included female speakers, and often an important part of these meetings was testimony from fugitives, detailing the horrors of slavery. Frederick Douglass was one of the most popular antislavery speakers.

The old antislavery movement was dying, and a new, more urgent, more aggressive national organization was taking its place. Abolitionists were speaking loudly and often. There was a new spirit with strong voices—black and white, male and female. Referring to slavery, William Lloyd Garrison said, "I do not wish to think, or speak, or write, with moderation. . . . I will not excuse. . . . I will not retreat a single inch—and I will be heard." He expressed the thoughts and feelings of many of his followers.

William Lloyd Garrison and other abolitionist leaders, c. 1866

Some Northerners saw slavery as a Southern problem and did not want to be bothered with it. Others were against slavery but were not necessarily abolitionists;

in fact, some were against the abolitionists and viewed them as crazy, radical troublemakers. There were also proslavery Northerners, especially those who were making money from some aspect of the slave trade. Angry mobs sometimes broke up abolitionist meetings.

By 1833 the antislavery movement had taken a new turn—the aim was not only to end slavery, but actually to free people whenever possible. So all the while that blacks had been using secret highways and byways, roads, and waterways that sometimes led to freedom, and while enslaved people knew where the safe houses were, where the help came from, and what it took to make a successful bid for freedom, they had been laying the tracks of the Underground Railroad. The archaeologists who conducted research on the Lott property have possibly retrieved material evidence of this historical period when Northern blacks—a number of whom had once endured slavery themselves—Southern runaways, and white radical abolitionists came together, fueling a stronger antislavery movement.

Missouri Compromise

As the American nation expanded, so did the controversy over slavery. When Missouri became a state in 1821, there were eleven free states and eleven slave. Missouri's statehood upset the balance, because many of its settlers were Southern slave owners, and wanted to enter the Union as a slave state. To maintain the balance, Congress admitted Maine as a free state and drew an imaginary line along Missouri's southern boundary. Slavery would be allowed south of that line, but nowhere else in the Louisiana Purchase. The compromise did not end the strife over slavery, however. Southerners still felt that the government had no right to decide which states should be free or slave. The free states were upset that slavery had spread into the Missouri territory. The balance was fragile, and abolitionists tried to tip the scales.

The *Narrative of Thomas Smallwood* reflects a more radical side of the abolitionist movement. Smallwood's narrative describes how he, a freedman, working along with Charles C. Torrey, a white minister, attempted to rescue slaves from Washington and Maryland. The events he described took place around 1843. Torrey was among only a handful of white abolitionists who attempted slave rescues out of the South.

> On Monday we started for Wilmington, Delaware, and arrived there the same day, and put up at that excellent gentleman's, Mr. Thomas Garrot's [Garret]. The next day, Tuesday, we put out for Gannet's Square in Pennsylvania; there we obtained a waggon and span of horses and proceeded the same day for Maryland, and in the night, of the same day, reached a tavern near Mason's and Dixon's line [an imaginary line on the border between Delaware and Pennsylvania considered to be the boundary between the Northern and Southern states]. Early the next morning we were off again for Baltimore, and after driving all day and late at night, we arrived in Baltimore, at about eleven o'clock. The next morning we expected the four families we had written for. I therefore set out in pursuit of them, in the direction of the dock, where the Steamboat from Washington lay, and met two of them, the other two having declined to come. After making the necessary arrangements for their departure to Philadelphia, we again started for Washington at two o'clock the same day, and arrived there at eleven o'clock the same night, and stopped at friend John Bush's who had, according to our request, made the necessary arrangements for carrying out the enterprise. We kept ourselves very close the next day, intending to start at night with our chattels, about fourteen in number, but unfortunately for us the police of that city had been made aware of our coming, therefore while I was harnessing the horses in the stable, and Mr. [Torrey] was storing the people in the waggon, a friend came to me, and said, "friend Smallwood, I see some white men standing out there on the hill side

A

NARRATIVE

OF

THOMAS SMALLWOOD,

(Coloured Man:)

GIVING AN ACCOUNT

OF HIS

BIRTH—THE PERIOD HE WAS HELD IN SLAVERY—HIS.
RELEASE—AND REMOVAL TO CANADA, ETC.

TOGETHER WITH

AN ACCOUNT OF THE UNDERGROUND RAILROAD.

WRITTEN BY HIMSELF.

Toronto:

PRINTED FOR THE AUTHOR. BY JAMES STEPHENS, 5, CITY
BUILDINGS, KING STREET EAST.

1851.

and they look like constables." I immediately communicated the same to Mr. [Torrey], who said to me, I will go and see; he soon returned to me trembling, and saying they were constables and requested me to try and get the people out of the waggon, they were ten in number; but he soon said to me, you can't, they are closing on us; therefore we had to make speed in making our own escape and leave the poor creatures to the mercy of the bloodhounds.

—*from* A Narrative of Thomas Smallwood (Coloured Man!), Giving an Account of His Birth—The Period He Was Held in Slavery— His Release—And Removal to Canada, Etc., Together with an Account of the Underground Railroad Written by Himself.

Chapter 7

"Midnight Seekers after Liberty"
Anecdotes and Memories
Uncover the Past

5 mo. 8 - A colored man and wife from Mason Co. Kentucky - 2

5 mo. 10 - A colored man from Winchetta [?] Kentucky

5 mo. 25 - 4 colored men from Mason Co. Kentucky, one of them taken in Woodbury - 4

5 mo. 27 - 3 colored men - from Mason Co. Kentucky

6 mo. 4 - 3 colored men from Tremble [?] Co. Kentucky and 1 white man from Vixburg Mississippi - 4

6 mo. 15 - A colored man from Kentucky driving carriage for an Oberlin lady - 1 . . .

8 mo. 16 - A colored man and wife and one child . . . and wife's sister from Kentucky—the man having been back from Gilead for them - 4 . . .

> 8 mo 24 - A colored woman who had been to Canada and went
> back and got four of her children and one grandchild/and a man
> and wife from Kentucky - 7

The above is a sampling of diary entries that Daniel Osborn, a Quaker living in Alum Creek Settlement in Delaware County, Ohio, made in a five-month period in 1844. All that remains of the diary is a single sheet of paper written on both sides. Few people kept such records. Perhaps Osborn wrote this list for the same reason that we all write down information and make lists—so that we do not forget.

But the list was a rare and important find for Wilbur Siebert, a historian and college professor who wrote the monumental study *The Underground Railroad from Slavery to Freedom*, published in 1898. In this chapter we will see the ways in which Siebert and another nineteenth-century researcher, William Still, used evidence to write books about the Underground Railroad. Whereas Siebert collected and weighed information of all kinds to tell everything he could about the Railroad, Still concentrated on recording firsthand accounts of escaping slaves in an attempt to put a human face on their history.

Diary entries like Daniel Osborn's give little information. There are no names or physical descriptions. There is no indication of the route the runaways took as they made their escape or where they were headed once they left Alum Creek. Or did they remain at the settlement? Probably not. Law enforcement looking for fugitives would seek out Quaker settlements near the Kentucky-Ohio border.

Yet, even though Osborn's entries are brief, they show a pattern. Most of the runaways were male, but women and children traveled the road, too. The groups of people were small, no larger than seven. Two of the fugitives had successfully escaped but returned to the South for loved ones. Most of the runaways were from Kentucky. Just as fragments of wood and shards of glass can yield important

Ripley, Ohio

Situated in Brown County, Ohio, Ripley was a freedom zone for slaves escaping across the Ohio River from Kentucky. Two of the best-known antislavery workers in Ripley were John Rankin and John P. Parker. Rankin, a Presbyterian minister, was active in the antislavery movement. His home in Ripley, sitting at the top of a hill that could be seen by people escaping across the river, was a refuge and hiding place for runaways. It was said that the light of a lantern in the window of the Rankin home, as well as other homes on the north shore of the Ohio River, was a signal that runaways could find help there. John Rankin and his wife, Jean, helped refugees from slavery from 1825 through the Civil War. The house is now a historic landmark.

John P. Parker purchased himself, paying $1,800 to the Mobile, Alabama, man who owned him. He left the South in 1845 and settled in Ripley. Parker was a skilled ironworker and opened a foundry in the 1850s. Parker conducted his own Underground Railroad work. It was said that almost every night he would row over to the Kentucky side of the river looking for enslaved men and women trying to reach the Ohio side. In doing so, Parker risked being caught, which could mean either reenslavement or ten to twenty years in the penitentiary.

information at an archaeological site, this piece of paper, too, sheds a faint light on the hidden past.

Based on Osborn's notes and an interview Siebert held with another person from the Alum Creek Settlement, Siebert made generalizations about the number of runaways who may have escaped to Ohio. Osborn helped forty-seven people from April to September 1844. The other person from Alum Creek claimed to have helped sixty runaways during the year 1854–55.

Estimating that the greatest period of Underground Railroad activity may have been the years 1830 through the beginning of the Civil War in 1860, and taking 1844 as an average year for numbers of people escaping into Ohio, Siebert reasoned that "not less than" 40,000 fugitive slaves passed through Ohio. It is only an estimate, and as Siebert warns his readers, we must be careful with numerical generalizations.

Siebert provides other interesting information about the numbers of people who ran, even though it is impossible to say definitely how many people escaped into Canada or how many were helped into the North. For example, an Ohio man who aided runaways said that on one occasion he fed twenty fugitives. Another person named four families in southern Ohio who claimed that they sent a thousand fugitives to Canada before 1817.

A man in Lancaster County, Pennsylvania, reportedly helped slaves for fifty-six years. Like so many others, he did not keep records, but it was estimated that between the years 1824 and 1853, when he passed away, he had helped approximately thirty-five men and women a year in their attempts to escape slavery.

All of these accounts are hearsay. Yet, even though we have no way of verifying the numbers, they do give us some idea of how many people attempted to reach the North.

Siebert interviewed a woman who claimed that John Fairfield, a white Southerner, helped not "only hundreds, but thousands" of slaves to freedom. A Princeton, Illinois, man reported that his greatest success in helping fugitives was aiding thirty-one men and women in six weeks' time. Another person said that he helped 103 people get to Canada in 1852. In Quincy, Illinois, near the slave state of Missouri, a resident said that during a period of twenty-five years he assisted "some two or three hundred fugitives." If he helped 300 people over a twenty-five year period, that would amount to twelve persons a year. Again, although all this evidence is anecdotal, it strengthens our impression that a good number of slaves received help on their journeys to the North.

"Freedom Stairway." Some of the enslaved men and women who escaped across the Ohio River into Ripley, Ohio, climbed these hundred steps leading from the river to John Rankin's house. The stairway no longer exists. Photo c. 1910.

When Wilbur Siebert researched information about the Underground Railroad, he had the advantage of being able to interview people who had actually experienced the events about which he was writing. He received correspondence from Frederick Douglass, for example, and had a personal interview with Harriet Tubman in 1897. He communicated with many other abolitionists, black and white, as well.

Siebert called upon eyewitnesses to Underground Railroad activity, even though age might have dimmed their sight and in some cases their memories. The people he interviewed were recalling events that had occurred thirty and forty years in the past. In a sense some of his interviews are similar to slave narratives. People were recalling events that they had experienced firsthand, relating family oral history, or remembering what they knew just from having lived during a specific historical period. A number of the people who responded to Siebert were children when certain events occurred. A Columbia University professor wrote to Siebert in 1896, relating an incident from his childhood:

> *The first clear, conscious memory I have is of seeing slaves taken from our garret near midnight, and forwarded towards Sandusky. I also remember the formal, but rather friendly, visitation of the house by the sheriff's posse.*

Although the bulk of Siebert's research is based on these recollections and narratives, he made every effort to corroborate the information he received. A man from Northwood, Logan County, Ohio, wrote the professor a letter dated September 22, 1894:

> *In Northwood there is a denomination known as Covenanters; among them the runaways were safe. Isaac Patterson has a cave on his place where the fugitives were secreted and fed two or three weeks at a time until the hunt for them was over. Then friends, as hunters, in covered wagons would take them*

to Sandusky. The highest number taken at one time was seven. The conductors were mostly students from Northwood. All I did was to help get up the team.

A minister from Pennsylvania who did not know the other letter writer told the same story:

In 1849 my brother . . . and I went . . . to Logan Co., Ohio, to conduct a grammar school . . . at a place called Northwood. . . . The region was settled by Covenanters . . . and every house was a home for the wanderers. But there was a cave on the farm of a man by the name of Patterson, absolutely safe and fairly comfortable for fugitives. In one instance thirteen fugitives after resting in the cave for some days, were taken by the students in two covered wagons to Sandusky, some 90 miles, where I had gone to engage passage for them on the Bay City steam boat across the lake to Malden—where I saw them safely landed on free soil, to their unspeakable joy.

Another letter described activity in southern Illinois:

The fugitives came up the river to Chester, Illinois, and there they started northeast on the state road, which followed an old Indian trail. The stations were each in a community of Covenanters.

Even though anecdotes like these cannot automatically be taken for fact, they become much more significant as evidence when the details are repeated in the same way by independent sources.

Siebert gathered evidence for five years. He compared the data he found in published books and articles with the anecdotes and the information people gave him. He read magazine and newspaper articles written in the 1870s,

1880s, and 1890s recalling the days and incidents related to the Underground Railroad.

Because of the need for secrecy, he explained, there were few records. In learning the details of how fugitives were helped, the roads they traveled, the disguises they used, the places they hid, and the numbers of people involved, Siebert depended on the memories, anecdotes, and oral histories of people who were still living.

From his sources, Siebert concluded that the work of helping runaway slaves was "spontaneous." The Underground Railroad was not a formal organization with officers, dues, and regular meetings. Like-minded people in a particular neighborhood who were willing to take a chance and help a runaway had to be prepared at a moment's notice to harbor a fugitive or show him or her how to get from one point to another.

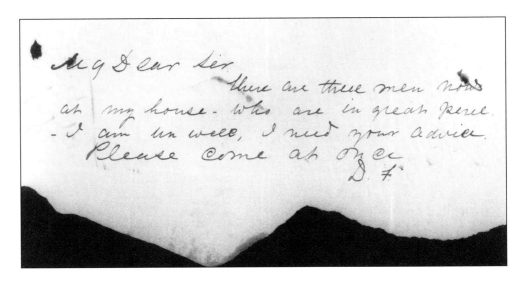

Note written by Frederick Douglass in 1857 to his neighbor, Samuel Porter. They and other abolitionist neighbors often helped runaways. The "three men in great peril" were probably fugitive slaves desperately trying to reach Canada.

Robert Purvis, a black abolitionist who was active in Philadelphia, concurred with Siebert. He wrote, "The funds for carrying on this enterprise were raised from our anti-slavery friends, as the cases came up, and their needs demanded it." Purvis went on to say that some fugitives needed only "advice and direction on how to proceed." He also added that his best workers were two Baltimore market women who directed fugitives to him. In his letter to Siebert, Purvis stated that in his Philadelphia home one room had a trapdoor in the floor, beneath which he had built an area to hold fugitives.

Siebert's inquiries did not always turn up information that confirmed the existence of the Underground Railroad. Thomas Wentworth Higginson, the Massachusetts abolitionist and commander of the first black regiment of the Civil War, informed Siebert in a letter written in 1896 that "there was no organization in Massachusetts answering properly to the usual description of the U.G.R.R." Was Siebert as puzzled as we are at this statement? Given the amount of evidence that slaves were regularly given safe passage in Massachusetts, we can only guess that what Higginson meant was that he knew of no formal organization named the "Underground Railroad."

Siebert's impression that the Underground Railroad was spontaneous and loosely organized was confirmed by other writers. James H. Fairchild, an abolitionist and at one time president of Oberlin College, said that although the Oberlin community was able to effectively help fugitives, there was little organization. Fairchild believed that the most organized areas had been in Cincinnati, Philadelphia, and Wilmington, Delaware—where the abolitionist Thomas Garrett claimed to have helped 2,700 runaways. He said that in those areas there were communities of free blacks who would shelter and hide fugitives while plans were made to get them to safety.

The Quaker Levi Coffin, who has been called "the president of the Underground Railroad," described how he began the work of aiding fugitives in

North Carolina. It was not organized at all, he said, but he was there for those who needed help:

> *Runaway slaves used frequently to conceal themselves in the woods and thickets in the vicinity of New Garden, waiting opportunities to make their escape to the North, and I generally learned their places of concealment and rendered them all the service in my power. . . . These outlying slaves knew where I lived, and, when reduced to extremity of want or danger, often came to my room, in the silence and darkness of night, to obtain food or assistance.*

It appears that wherever there was a lot of activity, there was more organization. We have already seen that communities of free blacks became safe havens for fugitives. By 1838 in Philadelphia and New York City, vigilance committees were formed for the purpose of making sure that a fugitive would not be arrested and that an enslaved person who wanted to escape would be helped. Frederick Douglass was directed to the New York Vigilance Committee when he arrived in the city in 1838. In the 1850s Boston, Massachusetts, and Syracuse, New York, also had vigilance committees.

One important function of the vigilance committees was to raise money. Money was needed to find temporary shelter for fugitives, to provide clothing and food, and in some cases to give them the fare for passage on ships or trains. By the 1850s, actual railroads were also used as a means of escape. Sometimes the work of the Philadelphia Vigilance Committee entailed meeting a train bringing an escapee from the South.

A runaway did not simply purchase a ticket. Someone had to help. The individual needed papers saying that he or she was free or a pass allowing the person to travel. The fugitive also needed money and had to be able to act as though he or she were accustomed to riding trains. Sometimes fugitives were hidden in freight cars.

Helping a fugitive escape via railroads is only one example of the kind of assistance that the vigilance committees provided. Various methods were employed in order to move fugitives from one point to another. Because every situation was different, there could not be one grand plan, with one or two grand escape routes.

Trains

In a letter written in 1860 to abolitionists in England, Frederick Douglass described how he helped fugitives use the trains. "They usually tarry with us only during the night, and are forwarded to Canada by the morning train. We give them supper, lodging, and breakfast; pay their expenses, and give them a half dollar over."

Based on the information he received, Siebert also tried to establish the actual routes that made up the Underground Railroad. He identified routes in Iowa, Wisconsin, Illinois, Indiana, Ohio, Michigan, Pennsylvania, New Jersey, New York, Connecticut, New Hampshire, Rhode Island, Massachusetts, and Vermont. He also mentioned a few routes leading to the North in North Carolina, Maryland, and Delaware.

Even though Wilbur Siebert took pains to verify the information he received, it is possible that his idea of established "routes" on the Underground Railroad was somewhat overstated. Someone who helped a few runaways, maybe only once or twice, could have identified the way the fugitives traveled as a route on the Underground Railroad. For example, one of the people responding to Siebert about activity in Maine identified a "branch of the Road running from Portland, Maine to Effingham, New Hampshire and north into Canada during the years 1843 to 1845." Another Portland resident said that "at one time after the passage of the second Fugitive Slave Law [1850] he cared for thirty fugitives."

It is quite possible that in fact some of these routes were used only as the need arose, and that there was no steady stream of runaways going through Maine, Vermont, or New Hampshire. We cannot know whether there were thirty fugitives or fifteen, because this testimony was based on memory, not on a list of runaways the person had helped. What we can surmise is that there were times when escaping slaves were taken to Canada via this route.

One person communicating with Siebert claimed that there were Underground Railroad lines running straight from the South to Canada. Because Siebert could not verify that statement, he included the information, but made no claim that these were regular routes.

Siebert was interested in reports that special signals and secret signs were sometimes used to indicate whether a route along the Railroad was safe for travel. Several people told Siebert that they remembered hearing a call like a hoot owl over the Ohio River when fugitives crossed from Parkersburg, in West Virginia. He said that there were different signals, such as different kinds of knocks on a door or window, in various neighborhoods: "In Harrison County, Ohio, around Cadiz, one of the recognized signals was three distinct but subdued knocks." When someone asked, "Who's there?" the answer would be "A friend with friends." People in another place might have used other signals. Passwords were used on some sections of the road. People in York in southeastern Pennsylvania used the code words "William Penn."

According to Siebert, few abolitionists went into the South to take out slaves. Fugitives had to get to the North before they were able to obtain help from the abolitionists and antislavery societies. Rather, it was primarily black people, both slave and free, along the southern borders of New Jersey, Pennsylvania, Ohio, Indiana, Illinois, and Iowa, who were able to assist fugitives to a free state. Sometimes they simply rowed runaways across a stream or told them how to reach the home of a friend who would help them.

Siebert tells of a free black man in Martin Ferry, Ohio, who often went to the Virginia shore to help slaves run away. The man acted drunk in order to disguise his intentions. All the while, he was giving out information on how to escape. Eventually law officers found out what he was doing, and he had to run to Canada himself to avoid jail.

Another of Siebert's many anecdotes tells of a black barber in the town of Jackson, Ohio, who rowed slaves across the river to Portsmouth. We're not told how often or how many times he did this—maybe only once or twice. A black man by the name of Wash Spradley of Louisville, Kentucky, is also mentioned. He is described as a shrewd person who helped many fugitives. Although it might not be possible to verify the details of these anecdotes, the number of such stories in Siebert's records strongly suggests that black people routinely acted as conductors along the Underground Railroad in the South.

Siebert worked with the information he had. The letters and statements he gathered from people who experienced the events we call the Underground Railroad give us an idea of what that period was like; Siebert's perspective and focus, however, were primarily on the activities of abolitionists and Quakers. Although he interviewed a few former fugitives, we get little sense of them as people—their desperation, fear, sadness, joy, loneliness, and other emotions growing out of their experiences.

Fortunately, we have a few written accounts, such as the famous narrative of Frederick Douglass, and that of William Wells Brown, who also escaped from slavery. There are other written narratives of people who are not as well known as Douglass and Brown: the *Narrative of Thomas Smallwood*, written in 1851, for

White Abolitionist Efforts in the South

In 1858 the radical abolitionist John Brown and a small company of followers went into Missouri and rescued an enslaved family. Although white abolitionists rarely entered the South in order to free slaves, according to some historians there had been other such incidents in the 1840s. Despite abolitionists' objections to direct action, three young white men in 1841 crossed the Mississippi River from Quincy, Illinois, into Missouri in order to rescue slaves. They were caught and sentenced to twelve years in the state penitentiary. In 1845 a white man living in Pensacola, Florida, was captured and punished for attempting to take slaves to the Bahamas. Rev. Calvin Fairbank also spent time in the penitentiary in Kentucky for his role in helping Lewis Hayden and his wife and son escape from Lexington, Kentucky. Hayden became instrumental in organizing the Boston Vigilance Committee.

example, and the *Narrative of J. W. Loguen*, an abolitionist and minister active in Syracuse, New York.

But what about the voices of other men and women who had freed themselves but were not literate and therefore could not write down their stories? Some of them told of their experiences under slavery, and their stories were written down for them. The abolitionists printed many of these stories in pamphlets and used them to show the rest of the world the horrors of slavery. The stories of many other fugitives were not told—unless they crossed paths with William Still between the years 1850 and 1860.

In 1872, William Still, a black abolitionist and chairman of the Philadelphia Vigilance Committee, published his book *The Underground Railroad*, one of the resources that Wilbur Siebert used in his study. Siebert called Still's book a "mine of material relating to the work of the Vigilance Committee of Philadelphia."

William Still's book is a treasure trove of articles, narratives, letters, and firsthand accounts of fugitives and those who helped them. Still's volume was published only seven years after slavery had ended—close to the time and events he describes. Not only did he hear accounts from people in the throes of running and seeking help, but beginning in 1850, he wrote down the information as it was given to him:

> *The risk of aiding fugitives was never lost sight of, and the safety of all concerned called for still tongues. Hence sad and thrilling stories were listened to, and made deep impressions; but as a universal rule, friend and fugitive parted with only very vivid recollection of the secret interview and with mutual sympathy; for a length of time no narratives were written.*

Despite the danger, William Still decided that he had to write down the stories, which had touched his heart. Fortunately for us, he did:

All over this wide and extended country thousands of mothers and children, separated by Slavery were in a similar way living without the slightest knowledge of each other's whereabouts, praying and weeping without ceasing . . .

Still assures the reader that he has not added to the narratives in his book. He says that "the most scrupulous care has been taken to furnish . . . simple facts,—to resort to no coloring to make the book seem romantic." The stories of slaves' lives and their flights to freedom did not need additional drama.

William Still knew that he was witnessing history and that these anecdotes and narratives and the correspondence to support them were too important to lose. He states that "he owes it to the cause of Freedom and to the Fugitives" and their descendants "to bring the doings of the [Underground Railroad] before the public in the most, truthful manner; not for the purpose of amusing the reader, but to show what efforts were made and what success was gained for Freedom."

Still also reminds us that his records cover activity in the Philadelphia region only and that there were many local branches of the Underground Railroad in different parts of the country. Even so, we can get an idea of what it must have been like to run with the "midnight seekers after liberty." The fugitives arriving at the Vigilance Committee's headquarters were representative of self-emancipated men, women, and children arriving in other parts of the North.

One of the many events William Still wrote about is the treacherous journey that four young men—William

---

Numbers

Occasionally, a worker on the Underground Railroad left written evidence of the number of fugitives he or she had helped. In a letter dated November 7, 1857, Elijah Pennypacker of Chester County, Pennsylvania, wrote to William Still: "Respected Friend: There are three colored friends at my house now, who will reach the city by the Phila[delphia] & Reading train this evening. Please meet them. We have within the past 2 mos. passed 43 through our hands, transported most of them to Norristown in our own conveyance." (From William Still's *The Underground Railroad*.)

Thomas Cope, John Boice Grey, Henry Boice, and Isaac White, slaves in Delaware—made to free themselves. On a Saturday night near the end of January, they decided to escape, no matter how dangerous the journey. The abolitionist Thomas Garrett in Wilmington had helped many a fugitive, but they probably knew nothing of Garrett or how to reach him. It appears that they were confined to the area where they had been enslaved and did not know how to escape by land. But they had always lived near the bay, and they knew that the free state of New Jersey was just across the water. So, as Still wrote:

> They finally decided to make their Underground Rail Road exit by water. Though they didn't know the way by water, either. Since they'd lived all their lives not far from the bay, they had some knowledge of small boats, skiffs in particular. . . . That evening as they stood on the beach near Lewes, Delaware and cast their longing eyes in the direction of the Jersey shore, they made the decision to steal one of the skiffs and leave. A fierce gale was blowing, and the waves were running fearfully high. . . .

But they were determined to be free and made a bold move:

> With simple faith they entered the skiff; two of them took the oars, manfully to face uncertain dangers from the waves. But they remained steadfast, . . . as they felt that they were making the last stroke with their oars, on the verge of being overwhelmed with the waves. At every new stage of danger they summoned courage by remembering that they were escaping for their lives.
>
> Late on Sunday afternoon, the following day, they reached . . . the Jersey shore. The relief and joy were unspeakably great, yet they were strangers in a strange land. They knew not which way to steer. True, they knew that New Jersey bore the name of being a Free State; but they had reason to fear that they were in danger. In this dilemma they were discovered by the captain of an

oyster boat whose sense of humanity was so strongly appealed to by their appearance that he engaged to pilot them to Philadelphia.

The boat captain took them to William Still at the Vigilance Committee. Was the captain part of the organized Underground Railroad system? Perhaps he was. He knew where to take the fugitives. Or, maybe he was one of the many people who, although not necessarily proclaiming themselves abolitionists, would help a runaway in distress whenever possible.

What makes William Still's account so interesting and alive is that he provides descriptions of people—at times touching, sometimes whimsical, at other times so precise we can "see" the people he is describing. For example, his descriptions of the four men who escaped help us to visualize them: "William Thomas, was a yellow man, twenty-four years of age, and possessing a vigorous constitution." Still says that John Boice Grey was "only nineteen years of age, spare built, chestnut color, and represented the rising mind of the slaves of the South." In other words, slaves were leaving the South in increasing numbers. "Isaac was

William Still, wood engraving by John Sartain, c. 1850s. When Still passed away in 1902, the New York Times referred to him as the father of the Underground Railroad. Like a good father, he tried to protect and help those who sought him out. Most important, he preserved the stories and history of people who had no voice.

twenty-two, quite black, and belonged to the 'rising' young slaves of Delaware."
Again, this is Still's way of saying that the young enslaved men and women in
Delaware were escaping.

One of the most important things that Still does in his book is give us some
insight into the hearts and minds of people who have been too often merely
described as slaves—things, victims, symbols, but not real people, like us. Grey,
the nineteen-year-old, told Still his reasons for leaving Delaware:

> *If you didn't do the work right, he [his master] got contrary and wouldn't give*
> *you anything to eat for a whole day at a time; he said a 'nigger and a mule*
> *hadn't any feeling.' . . . for some time his affairs had been in a bad way; he*
> *had been broke, some say he had bad luck for killing my brother. My brother*
> *was sick, but master said he wasn't sick, and he took a chunk, and beat on*
> *him, and he died a few days after.*

Grey was distraught over what had happened to his brother and thought that
he would be the next victim of his master's rage.

Isaac White explained to Still why he had left and why he would chance death
in a raging storm rather than remain in slavery: he was often beaten, and the last
time his owner beat him he tried to fight back, but the man, who was a blacksmith
and evidently quite strong, continued to beat White, practically killing him. White
was injured and helpless for two weeks. It was then that he promised himself
"to freedom and Canada, and resolved to win the prize by crossing the Bay."

Still does not say what happened to the four men, but we can guess that
they did not stay in Philadelphia or New Jersey. That would put them too close
to Delaware and the danger of their owners' claiming them.

In addition to recording the first-person accounts of fugitives who came his
way, William Still gives us samples of letters and correspondence relating to his
work on the Vigilance Committee. Like Siebert, Still was interested in the idea

A BOLD STROKE FOR FREEDOM.

Escaping Slaves, *men and women, wood engraving, C. H. Reed, artist, c. 1872*

that people involved in helping runaways used secret codes and signals. We learned that Siebert had noted the use of the code words "William Penn." Still gives us an example of a letter writer in Washington, D.C., looking after the welfare of some fugitive slaves, who signs his letter "William Penn":

Washington, D.C. 1856

Dear Sir:—I sent you the recent law of Virginia, under which all vessels are to be searched for fugitives within the waters of that State. . . . It was long ago suggested by a . . . friend, that the "powder boy" might find a better port in the Chesapeake bay, or in the Patuxent river to communicate with this vicinity, than by entering the Potomac river, even were there no such law. . . .

He goes on to tell of several women who are in great need of help:

. . . two have children, say a couple each; some have none—one can raise $50.00, another, say 30 or 40 dollars. . . . None of these can walk so far or

so fast as scores of men that are constantly leaving. I cannot shake off my anxiety
for these poor creatures. Can you think of anything for any of these? . . .

> *Yours,*
> *William Penn*

Although their methods and focus differed, both Wilbur Siebert and William Still left important research and records that can help us to better understand the historical phenomenon we call the Underground Railroad and to hear the voices of the people who were involved in its operation.

John P. Parker, a freedman who helped runaways cross the Ohio River into Ripley, Ohio, one of the more famous stops on the Underground Railroad, gave this somewhat humorous account of his first rescue. In spite of the humor, the danger is apparent.

> *My first experience with the runaways was in 1845 in Cincinnati, where I*
> *was working at my trade as an iron molder. I was in contact with the free colored*
> *men, so I knew of Levi Coffin, the Quaker who was active and resourceful.*
> *There are said to have been 22 fugitives hid away in his house at one time. . . . I*
> *had met a freeman who was a barber, in the house where I was living. He told*
> *me that he had lived in Maysville, Kentucky, and was under suspicion of having*
> *helped runaways. . . . The man confided in me that several nights before he*
> *was forced to get out of town, [he] met two girls in the act of running away.*
> *. . . He had made up his mind to run the girls away and proposed I accom-*
> *pany him back to Maysville to aid in the enterprise. . . . His plan was to go*
> *to a Ohio upriver town called Ripley of which I had never heard. . . . We*
> *would make our headquarters there instead of Maysville, where he was*
> *known. His plan was to follow up the river after night [and] steal a skiff, while*
> *I went into Maysville to get the girls. . . . At the appointed hour I was in the*

boat waiting. Shortly afterwards, two figures came stealthily down the bank. One was short, the other tall, but both were unusually fat. When the girls came to me I understood what gave them their unusual size. They had on not only their mistress' tilter hoops, one had on four dresses, the other confessed to three and much underwear. What to do with these two stuffed figures was a problem. . . . I finally arranged the matter by placing one in each end of the boat. . . . Any other time I would have laughed, but serious work, and dangerous work to me, was at hand. There was no time to lose as I had to row ten miles, and get the girls out of sight before daylight. . . . I rowed to the Ohio side, where I was more or less familiar. . . . Just before I reached Logan's Gap, a low pass through the high hills, I heard the rhythmical beat of oars back of us. . . . My only safety was ashore. I made the girls take off their extra clothing and throw them in the bottom of the boat. The girl in the bow became entangled in her hoop skirts and fell overboard with a yell that echoed in the hills. When I stopped to fish the girl out of the river, I lost one of my oars, so I had to paddle ashore. . . . By this time we could hear the frantic efforts of our pursuers distinctly, though I could not see them. At this point, while the bank was low, it was very steep. The tall girl clambered up the bank without much trouble, but the short one could not make it. She started to scream, but I slapped my hand over her mouth and threatened to strangle her, shutting her up in a hurry. Between the tall girl pulling and my pushing we got the girl up the bank, hoop skirts and all. . . . Clinging to a well-traveled road, I made the girls follow along this until daylight began to break. I knew we could not make Ripley, so I turned back, carefully concealing our trail where we left the road. I climbed halfway up the hill and hid in a clump of bushes. . . . [Parker and the girls hid all day until the evening.] Shortly after dark we arrived at the colored settlement on the side of the hill overlooking Ripley. . . . That was my . . . introduction to Ripley and the Underground Railroad.

—His Promised Land: The Autobiography of John P. Parker

Chapter 8

The Last Stop
Outrunning the Fugitive Slave Laws

At times, in order to find evidence of the Underground Railroad, we have to start at the end of the "line" and backtrack to the beginning. We have seen that the paths to freedom led some fugitives to the Caribbean and others into Mexico or to Native American territory, but Canada remains the symbol of the slaves' search for freedom. This vast land to our north has often been called the last stop on the Underground Railroad. For while the United States was enacting the Fugitive Slave Law of 1793, Canada also enacted a 1793 law that began to abolish slavery there.

Canada has become a rich resource for evidence of the Underground Railroad. Thanks to the preservation of various historical sites related to American fugitive slaves, we know what happened to these self-emancipated people once they reached Canada. Canadian researchers are making fascinating discoveries about the Underground Railroad, retracing the steps that fugitives took, through information in the archives of historical institutions and libraries in a number of Canadian and American cities and states.

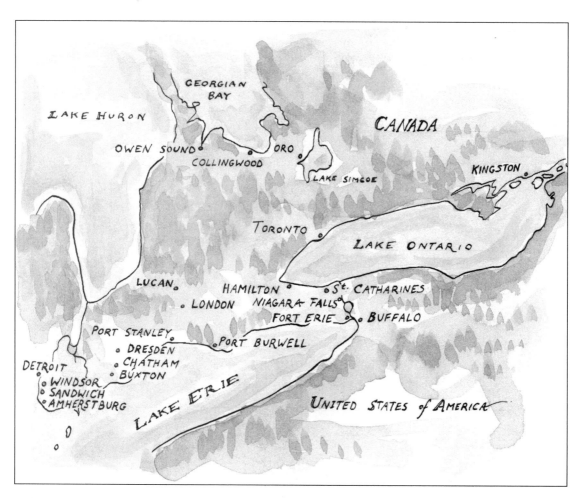

Refugee settlements in Canada

Some of the first black refugees to Canada went east to Nova Scotia after the American Revolution. Although a few also traveled all the way west to British Columbia, the vast majority went to present-day southwestern Ontario. The history of one of those refugees from slavery can be found in Ancaster, Ontario, in a simply constructed clapboard home now part of a tour of Underground Railroad sites in Canada.

Canadian Settlements

The Oro Settlement established in 1819 was among the earliest Canadian refugee settlements. A Canadian writer notes that remnants of this early settlement are found on the headstones in a small graveyard, and in an old log African Methodist Episcopal Church.

The best-known sites in what was called Canada West are Wilberforce, founded around 1830 with approximately 250 to 300 settlers who left Cincinnati, and the Dawn Settlement, founded by Josiah Henson and Quaker James C. Fuller in the early 1840s. The town of Dresden, Ontario, is built on this former settlement, but remains of the settlement can be found on the grave markers and in church and city records. Some of the descendants of this early settlement still live in Dresden, where Josiah Henson's home is a historic site open for tours. Across the river from Detroit, there were communities in Windsor, Sandwich, and Amherstburg.

One of the largest and most successful settlements was in Buxton, founded in 1849 by Rev. William King, a white Presbyterian minister, and fifteen former slaves. By about 1856, 2,000 black people lived there. Today there are about a hundred black families living in this farming community, but only three black farmers still work some of the land that their ancestors tilled. The 1861 one-room schoolhouse built by former slaves has recently been restored and is part of the Buxton National Historic Site and Museum.

Harriet Beecher Stowe

Harriet Beecher Stowe (1811–1896) was raised in a staunchly anti-slavery family. Stowe's book *Uncle Tom's Cabin,* published in 1852, exposed the horrors of American slavery to a wide audience, selling 300,000 copies in the first year of publication. Although written in the sentimentalized, melodramatic style of popular nineteenth-century literature, with stereotypical characters, the book's impact was phenomenal. *Uncle Tom's Cabin* may have made Northerners more sympathetic toward the abolitionist movement. The book was banned, however, and vilified as abolitionist propaganda in the South.

It is believed that the book's main character, Uncle Tom, was based on Josiah Henson, who escaped to Canada with his wife and four children in 1830. Henson returned to Kentucky and, like Tubman, rescued other slaves.

Engraving by Alonzo Chappel, 1872

The home once belonged to Enerals Griffin, who died in 1878. The descendants of Griffin and his wife, Priscilla, lived in the house until 1988. Family oral history combined with archaeology has given voice to people whose stories might otherwise have died with them.

According to the Griffin family oral history, Enerals Griffin was a slave in Virginia who escaped to the Niagara region of Canada in 1828 or 1829. Griffin married a woman who had also emigrated to Canada. It is believed that she was white. The couple had a son, James, and in 1834 they purchased the home in Ancaster, Ontario, which remained in the hands of their descendants for over 150 years.

When researchers conducted two archaeological digs in the four-room house, they found the usual artifacts you would expect in a comfortable nineteenth-century

The Griffin house, now a museum, has been restored to its pre–1850 condition.

home: pieces of ceramics, jewelry, and glass, and pages from magazines dating all the way back to the late 1800s. The most touching artifact they found was a lithograph under the paneling in a closet. The print was a copy of a popular and well-known 1859 painting entitled *Negro Life in the South*. Griffin, like so many others who ran, may have left loved ones back in the South. Evidently, he had not forgotten his roots. There might have been a part of him that continued to long for those he had left behind.

It also seems that he may have lent a helping hand to other fugitives who came to Canada. The archaeologist who conducted the dig on the Griffin house believes that Enerals Griffin opened his home to fugitives and that his home was similar to what we would call a halfway house today. Enerals Griffin offered shelter and helped refugees find employment and generally settle into their new environment. Perhaps he directed them to one of the black settlements in what was known at that time as Canada West.

Archaeologists and historians have uncovered other stories that end in Canada but have their beginnings in America. In 1985, archaeologist Karolyn E. Smardz organized a project for the Toronto Board of Education and discovered another Underground Railroad story.

Smardz organized a dig at the Sackville Street School, built in 1887. Smardz says, "It seemed like a good idea to go looking for immigrant housing under schoolyards in the inner city. The school board had to build schools where the highest number of immigrants lived and on the cheapest real estate they could get. They tore down some awfully humble housing, commercial establishments and early industrial properties to do it and graded the lots to form schoolyards. Then they laid down cinder bed and/or plank paving [that] sealed in

Remains of the color lithograph Negro Life in the South *found by archaelogists under the pine paneling in a closet of the Griffin home*

Negro Life in the South, *popularly known as* My Old Kentucky Home. *Oil painting by Eastman Johnson, 1859. This is how the lithograph would have looked when first displayed in the Griffin home.*

all those lovely remains under asphalt for years and years. Schoolyards are a great place to dig."

Smardz and the other researchers had to go back to public records and decide exactly where in the Sackville Street schoolyard they would dig. Looking at the *Toronto Street Directory of 1846* they discovered the following entry for lots 15 and 16: "Thornton Blackburn, cabman, coloured."

Who was Thornton Blackburn? Was he a descendant of one of the freed people who came to Canada with the British loyalists after the American Revolution? Was he the descendant of fugitive slaves from the United States or the descendant of Canadian slaves? Fascinated by this simple notation, Karolyn Smardz tried to find out whether there was more written information about Thornton Blackburn, cabman, coloured.

Smardz looked for additional historical documentation. Researching Toronto city directories, she discovered that Thornton Blackburn and his wife, Lucie, had resided in Toronto from 1834 to 1891 and owned the first taxicab company there. (These "taxis" were actually horse-drawn carriages.) Continuing her research, Smardz found Thornton Blackburn's grave marker in Toronto, providing a few more clues. The inscription on the tombstone showed that he had been born in Maysville, Kentucky. Like a detective, Smardz began to investigate the Blackburns' history seriously, traveling to Kentucky eight times. In an April 26, 2002, interview in the Louisville, Kentucky, *Courier-Journal*, Karolyn Smardz said that the Blackburns "were amazing people and I kind of got obsessed with them." Her research in Kentucky led her to Lansing, Michigan, where she found additional documentary information. Legal documents (depositions) in the Michigan Historical Center described the "Blackburn Riots of 1833" in Detroit and provided information about the Blackburns' escape from Kentucky.

Lucie and Thornton were not descendants of the black loyalists from America, nor were they descendants of Canadian slaves or of fugitive

American slaves. The Blackburns themselves had been fugitive slaves who had escaped to Canada.

Their journey began on a summer's night, July 3, 1833, in Louisville, Kentucky. Thornton and Lucie, each enslaved to different families, successfully emancipated themselves, escaping across the Ohio River into Jeffersonville, Indiana. The Ohio River was definitely a "freedom road" for Kentucky slaves. Posing as a free couple, they were allowed passage on a steamboat that carried them to Cincinnati, Ohio. Thornton's owner sent a male relative after them, but luckily Thornton and Lucie avoided the man who was hunting them down, caught a stagecoach to Sandusky, Ohio, and headed for Detroit, Michigan.

Thornton and Lucie Blackburn probably planned their trip carefully and knew the exact steps they would have to take to get out of Kentucky. They had papers saying that they were free. Perhaps these had been purchased. There were people who would forge passes and certificates of freedom for a fee.

In Detroit, the Blackburns were free and could live together without fear of being sold away from one another. But how free were they? The Fugitive Slave Act of 1793 was in effect in 1833 and gave a slave owner the right to reclaim his or her human property. But the law of 1793 in many cases was circumvented or merely ignored. If runaways were fortunate enough to reach free territory and find people who would help them, they might be able to make a clean escape.

It seems that the Blackburns followed an established pattern. They settled comfortably into Detroit's small black community in the free territory of Michigan. Thornton worked as a stonemason. Now he could keep the money he earned, and not give it all to his owner as he had had to do when he was enslaved.

But for Lucie and Thornton, Detroit was not far enough away from Louisville. Their owners found out that the couple lived in Detroit and sent a representative to reclaim them. When they were arrested and jailed for three days, however, Detroit's black community vowed to free them, saying that a person who had reached free territory should not be sent back to slavery. Black supporters rose up in a protest called the Blackburn riots. Antislavery whites joined the black community in helping the Blackburns escape from jail and took the couple across the Detroit River into Canada. But Amherstburg, a town that fugitives had often fled to, was too near the U.S. border for the Blackburns' liking. They eventually made a home in Toronto and ran their successful taxi business. They never had children, but they left a legacy that should not be forgotten. The Blackburns, remembering their own struggles, helped other black runaways who had made it to Canada.

By 1850, almost twenty years after the Blackburns made their journey, the passage of the harsher Fugitive Slave Law brought people to Canada who had been living in the North for many years. The Blackburns and other people who aided fugitives from slavery had a lot of work to do. Historical records indicate that when the 1850 law was enacted, the numbers of refugees going to Canada grew. The law was retroactive and applied to people who had run away from slavery years before. The historian Benjamin Quarles wrote that "many runaway slaves living in the North had decided to take to the road again, this time to Canada." Even those who had been living as free men and women for as long as twenty years could be reenslaved under this law.

Referring to the 1850 law, the antislavery congressman Thaddeus Stevens of Pennsylvania advised runaways in the North to "put themselves beyond its reach." According to Benjamin Quarles's research of church records and other documents, people did put themselves beyond the reach of the 1850 law. In Boston, Massachusetts, a few days after the law was enacted, eighty-five members of the African Methodist Church left for Canada, and a smaller Boston congregation lost ten members. Forty members of the First Baptist Church left for Canada, and the remaining eighty-five raised $1,300 to purchase the freedom of two of its deacons. Another church with 141 worshipers lost sixty.

At a black church in Rochester, New York, the pastor and 112 church members went to Canada. Only two members of the congregation remained behind. The situation in Buffalo, New York, was no better, where 130 people left the Baptist Colored Church.

Two hundred black people in Pittsburgh, Pennsylvania, continued their Underground Railroad journey just before the 1850 Fugitive Slave Law was enacted, and another eight hundred left in the succeeding years. Columbia, Pennsylvania, near the Susquehanna River and often a refuge for runaways, had a black population of 943 in 1850. Over a five-year period after the law was passed, 487 people from this community fled to Canada.

Commenting on the effects of the Fugitive Slave Law, William Still wrote, "Pennsylvania was considered wholly unsafe to nine-tenths of her colored population." And Harriet Tubman could no longer leave her charges in the North, but had to take them all the way to Canada.

Harriet Tubman (1820–1913) was another famous fugitive from slavery and a remarkable woman. Tubman has been called the Moses of her people. After escaping from a Maryland plantation in 1849, she returned to the South at least fifteen times to rescue others, including all of her family members. Tubman was a deeply religious, selfless woman who helped people all of her life.

When Tubman was in Canada, she attended the St. Catharines B.M.E. Church. Archaeologists are presently researching the church and the small house behind it where it is believed Tubman lived in the 1850s and where some of the refugees she brought to Canada stayed when they first arrived.

We can assume that many of those who continued their Underground Railroad journey were fugitive slaves who feared recapture. Not all of these emigrants were slaves, however; some were free, but saw the law as a noose around their necks. It dampened the spirits of those who had thought that slavery in America would eventually end. Mary Ann Shadd, for example, was an educator and journalist born into a comfortable free black family in Wilmington, Delaware. The family moved to Pennsylvania so that Shadd and her siblings could attend school. Though she was a successful, well-educated woman, she too left for Canada in 1850, believing that there was no hope of attaining full integration in the United States.

Fortunately for the refugees running from the fugitive slave laws, there were black settlements in Canada to take them in. Today, some of these former settlements are rich in archaeological and documentary evidence relating to the Underground Railroad. Just as Karolyn Smardz found information about Thornton Blackburn on his grave marker, there are headstones in small graveyards and church records in Canadian townships that are waiting to be rediscovered so that this Underground Railroad history can continue to be unearthed in the land of the North Star.

In his WPA interview, Arnold Gragston described helping runaways escape across the Ohio River, on the way north to Michigan and Canada:

> I don't know how I ever rowed the boat across the river the current was strong and I was trembling. I couldn't see a thing there in the dark, but I felt that girl's eyes.
>
> I was worried, too, about where to put her out of the boat. I couldn't ride her across the river all night, and I didn't know a thing about the other side.
>
> I don't know whether it seemed like a long time or a short time, now—it's so long ago; I know it was a long time rowing there in the cold and worryin'.

But it was short, too, 'cause as soon as I did get on the other side the big-eyed, brown-skin girl would be gone. Well, pretty soon I saw a tall light and I remembered what the old lady had told me about looking for that light and rowing to it. I did; and when I got up to it, two men reached down and grabbed her. . . . Then, one of the men took my arm. . . . "You hungry, Boy?" is what he asked me. . . .

That was my first time. . . . I found myself goin' back across the river, with two and three people, and sometimes a whole boatload. I got so I used to make three and four trips a month. . . . After that first girl—no, I never did see her again—I never saw my passengers. It would have to be the "black nights" of the moon when I would carry them, and I would meet 'em out in the open or in a house without a single light. . . .

There in Ripley was a man named Mr. Rankins. . . . Mr. Rankins had a regular "station" for the slaves. He had a big lighthouse in his yard, about thirty feet high and he kept it burnin' all night. It always meant freedom for a slave if he could get to this light. . . .

Finally, I decided to take my freedom, too. I had a wife by this time, and one night we quietly slipped across and headed for Mr. Rankins' place. . . . I didn't stay in Ripley, though; I wasn't taking no chances. I went on to Detroit and still live there with most of 10 children and 31 grand children. . . .

The bigger ones don't care so much about hearin' it now, but the little ones never get tired of hearin' how their grandpa brought Emancipation to loads of slaves he could touch and feel, but never could see.

Chapter 9

A Mystery
When History Keeps a Secret

Ｈow close are we to the distant past? Sometimes we may be much closer than we realize, especially when we are in a building that was constructed two centuries ago. Old buildings often hold secrets of the past; the challenge is to unlock them. In 1989 a Syracuse, New York, businessman, Vaughn Lang, stepped into the past when he purchased an old church building that was once known as the Wesleyan Methodist Church.

Lang had planned to completely remodel the 1847 structure, turning it into office space. His plans included excavating the basement and using it for storage. With his architectural drawings in place and just as he was preparing to gut the entire basement, he made a shocking discovery.

In a dark tunnel in one section of the basement, he saw what appeared to be images of faces baked onto the earthen wall. Lang realized that if he excavated the basement, he might be destroying something rare and important. Sensing that the images had value and perhaps historical significance, he postponed the excavation temporarily.

Instead of digging out the basement, he contacted archaeologists from Syracuse University to find out whether they could unravel the mystery of the faces on the walls. The archaeologists felt that Lang's discovery could be very

Historians in the Syracuse area suggest that this might be a representation of Frederick Douglass because of the hair and because Douglass's assumed birth date was etched into the bottom of the face.

This image depicts the tightly curled hair of Africans and African Americans.

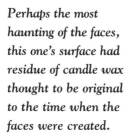

Perhaps the most haunting of the faces, this one's surface had residue of candle wax thought to be original to the time when the faces were created.

important and wasted no time in trying to find out everything they could about the underground art. Most of all, they did not want to lose the images before they could discover who had created them. Were they the work of one artist or several? Why was the art created? When were these images so carefully molded onto the basement walls of the church? Most of all, the archaeologists wanted to preserve them.

One of the first things the archaeologists did was to research oral as well as written documentation about the Wesleyan Methodist congregation. Although they were able to examine a great deal of historical material about the church, there was no mention of the art.

Fortunately, there were older people who remembered seeing the faces when they were children. Like the narratives and oral histories collected by Wilbur Siebert, William Still, and other writers and historians, recollections of people who had seen the faces provided valuable information.

Several people recalled that when they were children they went into the church basement and the tunnel and saw the faces. One eighty-three-year-old woman was a child of six when she, along with other children, entered the basement through a trapdoor. She recalls that the tunnel was dark, so she could not actually see the faces, but she felt them when she touched the wall: "We ran our hands across them, but we did not know that they were faces. We would have been too scared."

The information she provided helped the archaeologists begin to identify a time frame. Based on her age at the time of the interview, they learned that the art had been on the wall at least by 1923. Another woman also remembered the faces. She recalled going into the church basement in the 1940s at a Halloween party for children and seeing the sculptures in one area of the tunnel. She was told that the church's janitor had created the faces to pass the time while tending the coal furnace. A third person also remembered going into the church's basement in the 1940s and said that the images were created for a Halloween party for the Sunday school children.

There is, however, another story about the meaning of these faces in the church basement—a story that was forgotten by the 1940s. Researching the records of the Onondaga Historical Association, the investigators found a newspaper article published in 1933 in which one of the church's pastors tells of stories he had heard about the faces back in the late 1800s when he first became pastor at the church. Older members of the congregation had spoken of slaves being "hidden beneath the church," he said, adding that "hollow places in the earth below the floor are believed to be the original hiding places."

Is it possible that the art was created by fugitive slaves hiding in the church basement? This 1933 clipping was the only written documentation the archaeologists found that mentioned anything about the church's use as a stop on the Underground Railroad. Nothing was said about the faces on the wall.

Historical records, however, show that Syracuse, New York, was a hotbed of abolitionist activity. It is almost certain that this church, along with other churches and homes, was used as a station on the Underground Railroad. Like the Quakers, the Wesleyan Methodists were against slavery. The first minister of the Syracuse Wesleyan Methodist Church, Luther Lee, was an outspoken antislavery activist. Jermain Loguen was another abolitionist who worked to make Syracuse "safe" for fugitives.

Loguen had freed himself from slavery in Tennessee and escaped to Canada, but finally settled in Syracuse in 1841, just a few years before the Wesleyan congregation built the church in downtown Syracuse. He was the manager of the Fugitive Aid Society and was instrumental in helping fugitives obtain work. He wrote powerful letters to newspapers in the Syracuse area asking people to hire fugitives to work on their farms and in their businesses. The historian Benjamin Quarles has said, "How many jobs he found for more than three hundred former slaves that passed through his hands cannot be known, but it earned for Syracuse the title of 'the Canada of the United States.'"

A minister, Samuel J. Mays, recalled Loguen and his work on the Railroad. "In his hospitable home, was fitted up an apartment for fugitive slaves, and, for years before the emancipation Act, scarcely a week passed without some one, in his flight from slavedom to Canada, enjoyed shelter and repose at Elder Loguen's."

The Syracuse Vigilance Committee was well organized and active. It is more than likely that the Wesleyan Methodist Church formed the network of safe houses, churches, farms, stores, and businesses that was a part of the Underground Railroad in Central New York State.

Still, the question remains. Who created the faces? Were they made in the 1920s by a bored church janitor tending the furnace? Were they created for the amusement of the children at a Halloween party in the 1940s? Or, were they sculpted by fugitive slaves as they waited for passage to Canada? Maybe these faces were the images of loved ones they would never see again.

The archaeologists had quite a task on their hands as they tried to unlock the secrets of this purposely hidden past. They began by visiting the church and taking pictures in order to document the faces and the basement area where they

The Wesleyan Methodist Church. The steeple was added during reconstruction of the church in the late 1800s, presumably after the faces were created.

had been found. They also looked at the original building plans, noting the additions to the church since it was first erected in 1847. Two destructive fires in the nineteenth century had left their marks on the original structure. As a matter of fact, twentieth-century additions and changes practically masked the church's nineteenth-century beginnings. From 1857 through 1997, the building had undergone many alterations.

When the archaeologists entered the building, they went into the basement of the church—the modern section, probably built in the 1930s. Vaughn Lang led them to a large metal door painted black. Because there was no electricity in the section of the basement behind the door, Lang lit their way with a flashlight, throwing eerie shadows along the walls. The first thing they saw was a large ramp made of earth, which they had to climb to reach the tunnel. The space was small and confining—a tall person would have to bend while walking up the earthen ramp and remain that way walking toward the tunnel.

The researchers followed Lang's flashlight closely, for without it they would have been in total darkness. They found tool marks like those made by picks, shovels, and other hand tools. The space was disorienting, and it was difficult to be sure exactly where to step. Eventually, they stopped at a wall containing one of the faces.

The image was extremely deteriorated, with very few features resembling a face. Vaughn Lang also showed them a small section of the wall that appeared to be a face in progress. As he panned his flashlight around the space, they noticed that the tunnel turned off to the right before it continued. This was curious. Why didn't the tunnel continue on a straight course? There were no beams or anything else in the original structure blocking the passageway when it was dug out. What was the reason for this little jog? It could have been a decoy to throw off someone who was searching for fugitives hidden there. It seemed as though the tunnel had suddenly ended.

As their eyes became accustomed to the space, they began to see a little more of the tunnel's outline. They were still in a very confined area, too small to allow a tall person to stand up straight. The tunnel floor was very wet, because of water seeping into the basement.

The tunnel had a certain presence. Standing there, looking at the faces, the archaeologists sensed what a forbidding and difficult place this was and how uncomfortable it must have been to spend hours or perhaps even days there. The tunnel's humid air was difficult to breathe. Every movement and footstep in the main sanctuary of the church above could be heard through the furnace's old vent pipe. The researchers all stayed very still for a moment, imagining what a perfect hiding place this might have been.

They continued to walk and eventually came upon a long earthen bench. The tunnel then continued on a few more steps and opened into a spacious, circular area near the furnace, where there was no need to bend over. Here they saw more faces. The images were covered by a white, chalky film—salt. Syracuse has a high concentration of naturally occurring salts. The salts on the surface gave the faces a strange, ghostly quality; they had been preserved better than the faces outside this area, however, because they had been exposed to heat from a nineteenth-century fire.

The archaeologists began the actual dig. They removed wood, wallboard, and other debris. The earthen bench was near a storage area. Wood had been stored there in the nineteenth century, when a wood-burning furnace would have been in use, and coal was stored there in the twentieth century. They analyzed the bench. Although it could have provided a seat for someone watching the furnace, the archaeologists determined that it was too long to be only for seating and that it must have had some other purpose. Perhaps refugees sat and slept there. It was near the furnace, so it would have been warm. It was also raised off the damp floor.

Five of the faces were found in the circular furnace area, and the other two faces were on either side of the passageway where the tunnel seemed to end. All of the faces were created in the same way, first by gouging out pieces of the wall to create an oval support and frame and then by adding moist clay from the floor. The facial features were shaped and molded onto the wall. The hair appeared to be tightly curled like black hair. The archaeologists reported that "even where the hair appears to be parted and slicked back, characteristics of African hair were incorporated into the face by the artist." The artist used black ash to darken the clay and create dark eyes.

In their report the investigators note that the faces are different shapes and sizes, and that originally they must have had distinct features. Now, most of the faces are corroded and the images barely recognizable.

The next important step for the investigators was to determine as closely as possible the date of the section of the tunnel where the faces were found. As they excavated, the faces seemed to peer down on them. Along with recent refuse they found fragments of stained glass and nails dating back to the nineteenth century. They also found more stones from the original wall, which had been removed when the building was enlarged in 1857. The archaeologists believe that the evidence from historical documents supports the theory that the tunnel was dug in 1857.

Abolitionist activity was intense in Syracuse by 1857, and the need for secrecy was crucial. The Syracuse Wesleyan Church had grown by then and was active in the abolitionist movement. Its publishing activities were thriving as well. The church built a publishing house adjacent to the church building and published *The True Wesleyan*, an outspoken abolitionist publication. The atmosphere in Syracuse was more dangerous for a fugitive in 1857 than it had been in 1847 when the church was first built. Whereas there was no need for a secret tunnel in 1847, there certainly was a need for one by 1857.

The archaeologists carefully studied the layers of clay and soil to determine a date for the basement. The top layers of soil were composed of "burnt and hardened clay." Deeper layers changed to a mixture of sand and clay. They dug until they found part of a furnace. They were able to determine that the brick and ash came from an early wood-burning furnace—evidence that the tunnel was built before the Civil War.

Other artifacts in the basement indicated that this area was used in the early years of the church. Archaeologists found fragments of a type of glass window that dated back to the years 1846 to 1877. Another important find was a piece of ceramic pottery made in England that was very popular in the United States by the 1850s. This is strong evidence that the faces could have been there as early as 1857. In their search for information, the archaeologists were able to piece together still more of the puzzle in a surprising way. Two of the best-preserved faces had been baked in an 1898 church fire, which not only helped to protect them, but also offered clear evidence that those faces were created in the nineteenth century.

The question, though, still remains—who created the art? Amazingly, fingerprints were found on three of the best-preserved faces. They were not the prints of people who might have touched the faces in passing. The prints were embedded into the clay—left there by the person who was pushing and modeling it. The fingerprints were made by three different people, discounting the argument that the faces were created by one person.

The archaeologists report that we will probably never know who created this art or exactly when it was created, but evidence points to the nineteenth century. "Our research provides strong support for a nineteenth-century origin," they wrote, "and the historic context makes African American artists plausible. Even with strong inference, we can present no proof as to who actually made the art."

Ultimately, then, there is no way of telling who these artists were, or whether they were black or white, slave or free. The fingerprints of the artists will not be in any computer file; their DNA is not available for analysis. Maybe future scientists or historians will develop new techniques that will help them add to the story. But until then, the silent stone faces in Syracuse will continue to guard their secret.

Helping and harboring fugitive slaves in the 1850s was a serious federal offense, and the antislavery people in Syracuse and Central New York were the radicals of their time. Blacks and whites worked closely together for a common cause. Although their origins remain a mystery, the faces are, in a sense, appropriate symbols of a time and a place where some people defiantly chose to make a difference, and to leave behind a piece of art, a part of themselves.

The historical record shows us that Syracuse and other towns in Central New York saw a great deal of abolitionist activity. As early as the fall of 1839, a famous slave rescue case—similar to the Blackburns' in Detroit a few years earlier—occurred in Syracuse.

Harriet Powell, a young woman enslaved to a Mississippi couple, J. Davenport and his wife, traveled with the couple to Syracuse. They all stayed at the Syracuse House, a downtown hotel. Powell was so fair-skinned that at first the black employees of the Syracuse House thought that she was a white woman and a member of the family. When they found out that the beautiful young Southern woman was a slave, they offered to help her escape.

One newspaper account said that Powell wasn't sure at first, because she would be separated from her mother and sister back in Mississippi. Her situation did not seem as harsh as many others'. She was a "favored" slave who had no horror stories to tell. But she was still a slave. She decided to take the chance and escape. Although she knew her mother and sister would grieve for her, she

Anti-Slavery Meeting on the Common; *wood engraving, 1851, from* Gleason's Pictorial Drawing Room Companion, *May 1851*

also knew that her mother wanted her children to be free. "The greatest desire of my mother's heart was that her children might be free, and for that she prayed," Powell is quoted as saying.

She put her trust in Tom Leonard, a black waiter at the hotel. He in turn contacted people, white and black, who would help. On the evening of October 7, 1839, at a time agreed upon, Harriet Powell simply walked out of the home where a celebration was being held for the Davenports. Tom Leonard waited outside the house to carry her away. A farmer supplied the carriage that Leonard used to take Powell to a safe house, where she remained hidden for about a week.

Keeping one step ahead of her owner and the police, Powell was moved again until she finally reached the home of Gerrit Smith, the well-known abolitionist, in Peterboro, New York. In the meantime, Davenport had printed posters offering a $200 reward for her capture.

Powell was in Smith's home for only a few hours before Smith had one of his employees, Federal Dana, take her on her final journey to Canada. Davenport,

Reward poster for Harriet Powell

along with law officers, arrived at the Smith mansion eighteen hours after Powell had gone. The authorities knew that Gerrit Smith helped fugitive slaves, but this was 1839, so Smith was not fined or arrested.

By 1850, federal marshals were looking for fugitives, and stiff fines and jail sentences awaited anyone helping runaways; however, the harsher laws of 1850 did not deter the abolitionists and antislavery people in Central New York.

The struggle to abolish slavery was reaching new heights by the 1850s. The 1850 Fugitive Slave Law, which was seen as the long arm of the South reaching into the North, angered many Northerners and made them more sympathetic to the abolitionists. The law put enslaved people in a more desperate condition. Blacks who had emancipated themselves and who had been living in the North as free people for years were even more vulnerable to kidnappers and slave catchers.

On October 1, 1851, a black resident of Syracuse named William Henry, who called himself Jerry, was arrested and charged with being a runaway slave. Jerry had escaped from his Missouri owner and had been living and working in Syracuse. He was described as an exemplary citizen. At the time of Jerry's arrest, a large number of people were in Syracuse for the Onondaga County Fair, along with a number of abolitionists attending a political convention.

When word spread that a man had been arrested on suspicion of being a fugitive slave, the Syracuse Vigilance Committee and everyone else in town who had antislavery sentiments headed to the courthouse. Jerry was taken before Joseph F. Sabine, commissioner of the United States Circuit Court.

According to the law, Jerry was not allowed to testify in his own defense. He would be sent back to slavery in Missouri.

In all of the excitement and confusion as people descended on the commissioner's office, Jerry got away. Hindered by his shackles, he hadn't gone far before he was caught, beaten by the police, and carried to the jail. But this would not be the end of it. Abolitionists and other people sympathetic to Jerry defied the law and made a plan to rescue him.

A group of men, both white and black, broke into the jail, overpowering the guards. They took Jerry to the home of a black man, removed his chains, and then, to foil the police, hid him in the home of a white ally. After five days in hiding, he continued his journey.

Jerry received fresh clothing (another version of the incident says that he was disguised in women's clothing) and on October 5 was taken to the town of Mexico, New York, and the home of Orson Ames on Main Street. Because it was known that Ames, who was white, aided fugitives, Jerry was removed to the barn of Deacon Asa Beebe, where he hid for two weeks. Ames made arrangements in Oswego, New York, with one of the captains of the many merchant ships there. Jerry, hidden in a loaded wagon, left the Beebe farm at midnight on October 19 or 20. He was taken aboard a ship sailing for Kingston, Ontario.

After this incident, several of Syracuse's black abolitionists, including Jermain Loguen, had to go to Canada themselves until things cooled down. Samuel Ringgold Ward, a respected black religious leader, said that he had helped to remove Jerry's chains. He also headed for Canada. Loguen and four other blacks were indicted; however, of the eighteen men who were accused only three were tried. Until the start of the Civil War, New York State abolitionists celebrated October 1 as Jerry Rescue Day.

Another rescue incident was even more controversial. In the 1851 Christiana riot, a slave owner named Edward Gorsuch from Baltimore County, Maryland, went to Christiana, a southern Pennsylvania town, looking for several of his escaped slaves. Evidently Christiana had a black community that harbored runaways.

Gorsuch, with six other men, went to the home of William Parker, who had escaped from Maryland himself, and demanded that Parker let him come into his home to see whether the fugitives were there. Parker refused, and his wife, who was also a former fugitive, "blew a large dinner horn," a signal for other blacks in the area.

According to William Still, about thirty-five to fifty black men rushed to Parker's home armed with "guns, axes, corn-cutters, or clubs." Gorsuch and the men with him demanded that the suspected runaways come out of the house. The people in the house absolutely refused. They warned the whites to leave, saying that "they would die before they would go into slavery."

The argument between the two groups escalated, and two Quakers who lived nearby tried to calm the situation. The deputy ordered the Quakers to help him, a United States officer, capture the suspected fugitives. The Quakers refused to help, which under the Fugitive Slave Law was a crime. Shots were fired. Gorsuch was killed and his son wounded. The men with Gorsuch fled. Marines and a posse of civilians were sent to Christiana to restore order and make arrests. Blacks who happened to be in the area were caught up in the dragnet of police investigations.

Both men and women were arrested. Parker, his wife, and the slaves Gorsuch was searching for managed to escape and make it to Canada. Thirty-eight people, thirty-five of them black, were arrested for treason. Warrants were issued for the arrest of the two Quakers because they had refused to help the deputy marshal.

Return to Slavery

Like other highly charged cases tried under the fugitive slave laws, the attempted rescue and subsequent trial of Anthony Burns gripped the city of Boston, beginning on May 24, 1854. As Burns walked down a Boston street, he was arrested. The complaint presented to the U.S. district court charged Burns "with being a fugitive from labor and with having escaped from service in the state of Virginia." Riots ensued, and as a group of men, black and white, unsuccessfully attempted to rescue Burns, a man was killed. Boston's abolitionists publicized the case, several antislavery lawyers volunteered to defend Burns, and the black citizens of Boston raised $1,200, Burns's purchase price. His owner refused to sell him. On June 2, 1854, the commissioner of the district court ruled against Burns. U.S. marshals walked Burns to the wharf while military troops lined the streets to prevent people from rioting again. Burns boarded a steamer that returned him to slavery in Alexandria, Virginia.

John Brown

From the time John Brown (1800–1859) was a young man, his father taught him that slavery was a sin and that all people had the right to be free. Brown, a deeply religious man—some said he was a fanatic—was also a radical abolitionist who devoted his life to the antislavery cause. In 1854 Brown moved to the Kansas territory with his family and became involved in antislavery violence there. Believing that the only way to destroy slavery was through direct confrontation, on October 16, 1859, he and a group of twenty-one followers, both black and white men, attempted to seize the federal arsenal at Harper's Ferry, Virginia. After a battle with government troops, a number of Brown's men died, including two of his sons. Brown was found guilty of treason and was hanged on December 2, 1859.

John Brown, lithograph, c. 1850s

JOHN BROWN.
LEADER OF THE HARPER'S FERRY INSURRECTION.

The Christiana case became one of the most celebrated court cases of its time. In the end, none of the accused was found guilty of treason. People would continue to defy the Fugitive Slave Law. Fugitives would continue to run and strike for freedom, and the animosity and the divisions that existed among Americans over the slavery issue would eventually tear the country apart.

Forces and events came together in the 1850s that spelled the beginning of the end of slavery: As the country grew and more territory was acquired, it was no longer possible to keep a balance between slave and free territory. With the acquisition of Kansas and Nebraska, the struggles between proslavery and anti-slavery forces became bitter and deadly. There was so much loss of life in Kansas that it became known as "bleeding Kansas." In 1854 Congress passed the Kansas-Nebraska Act, allowing the settlers in the newly acquired Nebraska territory to decide whether slavery would be allowed. The passage of this bill upset abolitionists, who felt it encouraged the spread of slavery.

The Dred Scott decision was another blow to the antislavery cause. Dred Scott was enslaved to an army surgeon who took him to Illinois, a free state, and then to Wisconsin, free territory. In a case that was ultimately decided by the Supreme Court, Scott sued for his freedom. In an 1857 decision, Chief Justice Roger B. Taney ruled that Scott could not sue in a federal court because blacks were not citizens, and that residence in a free state or territory did not make a slave free.

John Brown's raid on Harper's Ferry in 1859 was yet one more violent event that seemed to foreshadow the beginning of the Civil War in 1861, which would ultimately end slavery in the United States.

William Wells Brown was born into slavery in Lexington, Kentucky, in 1814. A contemporary of Frederick Douglass, he was a famous antislavery lecturer as well as a novelist and a physician. Brown often dreamed of escaping to Canada, and on January 1, 1834, he quietly left the steamboat where he worked as a steward and stepped onto free territory, Cincinnati, Ohio, successfully emancipating himself.

I was hired to Capt. Otis Reynolds, as a waiter on board the steamboat Enterprise. . . . This boat was then running on the upper Mississippi. My employment on board was to wait on gentlemen, and the captain being a good man, the situation was a pleasant one to me;—but in passing from place to place, and seeing new faces everyday, and knowing that they could go where they pleased, I soon became unhappy, and several times thought of leaving the boat at some landing place, and trying to make my escape to Canada, which I had heard much about as a place where the slave might live, be free, and be protected. . . . During the last night that I served in slavery I did not close my eyes a single moment. When not thinking of the future, my mind dwelt on the past. The love of a dear mother, a dear sister, and three dear brothers, yet living, caused me to shed many tears. . . . At last the time for action arrived. The boat landed at a point which appeared to me the place of all others to start from. I found that it would be impossible to carry anything with me but what was upon my person. I had some provisions, and a single suit of clothes, about half worn. When the boat was discharging her cargo, and the passengers engaged carrying their baggage on and off shore, I improved the opportunity to convey myself with my little effects on land. Taking up a trunk, I went up the wharf, and was soon out of the crowd. I made directly for the woods, where I remained until night, knowing well that I could not travel, even in the state of Ohio, during the day, without danger of being arrested. . . . After dark, I emerged from the woods into a narrow path, which led me into the main travelled road. But I knew not which way to go, I did not know north from south, east from west. I looked in vain for the North Star; a heavy cloud hid it from my view. I walked up and down the road until near midnight, when the clouds disappeared, and I welcomed the sight of my friend—truly the slaves friend—the North Star!

—Narrative of William Wells Brown, a Fugitive Slave, Written by Himself

Chapter 10

The Search Continues

Just as there was more than one road to freedom, we have learned that there is more than one path for us to follow as we search for evidence of the Underground Railroad. The integration of scientific, archaeological, and historical documentation on the Fort Mose project, for example, shows us how many tools are available for gathering information. The researchers literally left no stone unturned, utilizing many investigative methods, from space-age technology to an old-fashioned search of seventeenth- and eighteenth-century church records.

The archaeological information provided material evidence of the everyday lives of the people who left the Carolina colony and found their way to St. Augustine—so that we even know the kinds of foods they ate. Because the Spanish kept such extensive records on the Fort Mose inhabitants, and because the investigators on this project had access to scientific and archaeological tools, the researchers were able to give us a three-dimensional view of a people and a place that was almost lost in time, disappearing in a northern Florida marsh.

Not only can archaeology uncover the past, at times it can shed light on oral history that cannot be proved through documentary evidence. In the case of the Lott house in Brooklyn, New York, for example, archaeological findings supported a long-held family belief that slaves had been hidden in a secret room in the house. The archaeologists did find a room hidden behind a closet. While the existence of the room does not prove absolutely that the space was used as a hiding place for runaway slaves, given other documentary and physical evidence, there is a good possibility that the family oral history is correct.

It is not always possible to have at hand the kind of information and investigative tools used to recreate Fort Mose or to unearth the history of the Lott house. Sometimes historians and researchers find evidence corroborating historical events in very ordinary documents. Who would think that lists of names on ships' logs could confirm little-known historical events?

We learn from scholarly research and from documents in Britain and the United States that during the American Revolution some people of African descent offered their services to the British military in order to obtain their freedom. This information about blacks escaping to the British is usually not mentioned in books about the war. The struggle of enslaved people to free themselves during this war of liberation often gets lost in the larger story. Nevertheless, the inspection rolls of British ships leaving New York Harbor in 1783, with their plain and simple entries, provide evidence that a number of enslaved people took steps to emancipate themselves during the Revolutionary War.

Plantation records, including journals and diaries kept by slave owners, can also confirm larger historical events, even when from a limited perspective. For example, entries kept by a South Carolina slave owner surmising that his slaves had run away to the British is validated, in a sense, by the ships' logs. A historian could extend this research. There might be other diaries, notations in plantation journals, or legal claims filed in American and British courts seeking damages for the loss of property, including slaves, that name a man, woman, or child who left with the British. The inspection rolls or ships' logs of British vessels leaving New York Harbor are important documents.

Our bodies of law and legal documents offer historians a wealth of information. The Fugitive Slave Laws of 1793 and 1850 seem to bear out the continuing efforts of enslaved people to rebel. There would be no need of such laws if there were no fugitive slaves. The severity of the 1850 law possibly indicates that more slaves were successfully running into the free states—not just lying out for a few weeks in the woods and swamps.

Old court cases give evidence of people trying to emancipate themselves, and impress upon us the impossibility of reducing human beings to mere property. Court records such as petitions and affidavits tell us where people ran to, and in some cases give clues as to their reasons for running.

Legal documents also reveal the lengths that people took to find a road leading to freedom. Testimony in the 1825 South Carolina legislative records tells the terrible tale of the capture and killing of a mother and father who had escaped to the swamps with their children. The records also contain a petition written on behalf of a freedman and presented to the South Carolina legislature in 1829. A former slave was petitioning the court for the freedom of his children.

The Fugitive Slave Laws and petitions and other legal documents all provide evidence that enslaved people were rebelling against slavery. The first step toward a journey to the North and maybe even Canada was the decision to run away.

In their book *Runaway Slaves: Rebels on the Plantation*, the historians John Hope Franklin and Loren Schweninger use runaway notices from major Southern newspapers along with legal petitions and claims in order to present interesting statistical information on runaway slaves. We get an idea of the number of people running away during the periods 1790–1816 and 1838–1860. We are given information about the numbers of male and female runaways, their ages, and even physical descriptions.

While the statistics are not exact and only give us an idea of the number of people who ran away, the authors point out the usefulness of legal petitions and

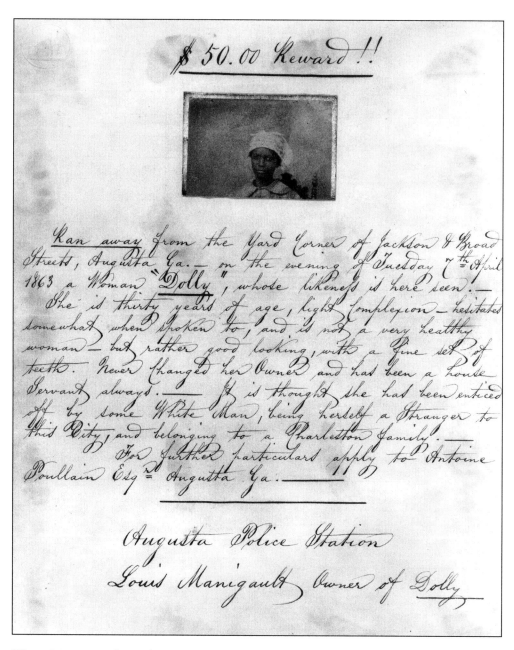

This 1863 poster shows that even during the Civil War, when there were thousands of escaped slaves and refugees, some people were still trying to find runaways and were using modern technology to do so. This is a rare runaway poster with a photograph.

runaway notices in their research: "Masters who advertised for a return of their property had little reason to misinform their readers and to be as precise as possible. . . . Responding to an event, situation, or potential danger, petitioners realized that it behooved them to be as forthright and candid as possible." The authors also state that in gathering information from court proceedings, the historian can analyze the responses of witnesses, defendants, and judges. At the same time, the writers remind us that "all sources are biased, but when it was in the interest of individuals to state their case as clearly and truthfully as possible and secure corroborating testimony, the primary source achieves a high degree of credibility."

Except for papers presented by black petitioners or, in many cases, presented by whites on behalf of the slave, the legal documents do not reflect the point of view, much less the feelings and emotions, of the enslaved individual. For that we have to look to other sources emerging out of the hearts and minds of those who lived through this period. Narratives both written and oral, autobiographies, biographies, anecdotes, and memoirs, despite their flaws, are where we might catch the voices of those who were there.

Although narratives, anecdotes, and memoirs are an important part of the research on the Underground Railroad, narratives such as the WPA interviews of slaves written in the 1930s and Wilbur Siebert's interviews of abolitionists years after the antislavery struggle ended cannot be taken at face value. Rather, they must be compared with other historical sources. Biographies and autobiographies have to undergo the same scrutiny. Sometimes a biography can tell us as much about the biases and prejudices of the biographer as it does about the life of the subject.

Even though William Still's anecdotes were from people who had recently used the Underground Railroad, it is quite possible that some of them might have exaggerated in order to obtain help, while others, out of shame or distrust, may have been hesitant to express how traumatic their experiences had been.

Even so, the anecdotes and the narratives are important to our understanding of the Underground Railroad.

Without the oral testimony of former slaves collected by historians, writers, and other researchers, we would have very little primary source material on the Underground Railroad. In a 1995 study of Railroad sites, the National Park Service confirmed the importance of the oral tradition in its research. The report emphasized, however, that the oral history "must be judged for reliability and balanced with customary research methodology." Although sometimes even careful and knowledgeable scholars cannot agree about the authenticity of individual slave narratives, that does not detract from their richness as a valuable resource.

Another rich resource relating to the narrative and oral tradition is the use of spirituals as a means of communication. Though the spirituals are essentially religious songs, they were also a form of communication among enslaved people. Not only did spirituals praise God, they also gave the singers a way of communicating their desires, their hopes, their feelings, and their opinions. Given the strong oral tradition among people of African descent, and the need for secrecy in order to survive, it stands to reason that some of the spirituals contained coded messages. Songs with double meanings were a part of the African oral tradition.

The evidence for the use of spirituals as a way of sending coded messages lies in the lyrics themselves, in understanding the oral traditions of Africans and people of African descent, and in the testimony of the slave narratives. Music was a powerful tool among enslaved African Americans. Why wouldn't they have used music to free themselves mentally as well as physically?

Sometimes, though, history keeps a secret. Even with all of the investigative tools, modern technology, and thorough research of documents, there are some things that we will never know for certain, for example, the identity of the creators of the faces in the church basement in Syracuse, New York. We can only make assumptions about who might have created them.

Another question that may never have a precise answer is, how many people successfully escaped to the North and to Canada on the Underground Railroad? The census figures of 1850 and 1860 report that only 1,011 slaves escaped in 1850, and 803 in 1860. (The report does not say where they escaped to.) The historian Wilbur Siebert disputes these numbers, however, wondering why slave owners insisted on a stricter fugitive slave law in 1850 if there were so few runaways.

In *Runaway Slaves*, the authors estimate that possibly fifty thousand slaves ran away annually; we have to keep in mind, however, that these runaways were often recaptured, and many of them were running within the South. The authors also estimate that after 1830 maybe one or two thousand slaves per year were able to reach the North, although there is no way of knowing exactly how many got on board the Underground Railroad. We do know, however, that four million men, women, and children were freed when slavery was abolished in 1865.

In the end, numbers do not really matter. From the evidence of the sources we have examined we have learned that while the Underground Railroad might not have been as we imagined it, with slaves escaping directly from

Redeemed in Virginia

By Catherine S. Lawrence. Baptized in Brooklyn, at Plymouth Church, by Henry Ward Beecher, May, 1863, Fannie Virginia Casseopia Lawrence, a Redeemed SLAVE CHILD, 5 years of age. Entered according to Act of Congress, in the year 1863, by C. S. Lawrence, in the Clerk's Office of the district Court of the United States, for the Southern District of New-York.

Photograph by Renowden, 65 Fulton Av. Brooklyn.

This portrait from 1863 shows five-year-old Fannie Virginia Casseopia Lawrence. The original caption reads, in part, "Redeemed in Virginia by Catherine S. Lawrence. Baptized in Brooklyn . . . by Henry Ward Beecher [Harriet Beecher Stowe's brother]." Catherine Lawrence was probably a relative, perhaps the child's mother. Up until the end of the Civil War in 1865, family members were finding one another, helped by abolitionists and other antislavery workers.

the South into the North with the help of Quakers and abolitionists in an unbroken, organized network of safe houses and depots that led to Canada, we do know that from the beginning of chattel slavery in colonial America to the end of slavery in 1865, there were routes and roads leading to freedom and there were people to help.

The Underground Railroad is very much an American story, symbolizing the will and courage to change one's situation even when it appears to be hopeless. It also represents the spirit of those who would constantly remind their fellow Americans of the principles of liberty and democracy on which the nation was founded.

Perhaps one of the most important lessons we can learn from these events in American history that we call the Underground Railroad is that the choices we make can effect change—one person chooses to run, and another chooses to help, even when he or she is in the same situation. There were abolitionists, black and white, who risked their lives, who went to jail, who were physically attacked because they defiantly broke the law on moral grounds. Perhaps the words of the Declaration of Independence, "All men are created equal," gave them the moral fortitude to defy the Fugitive Slave Laws. And there were slaves who could not be controlled and ran away time and again even when they were unmercifully punished.

The search for the Underground Railroad has not ended. There are still hidden rooms in old houses, and letters, diaries, memoirs, and family histories that researchers have yet to find. This is a "living" history waiting for a new generation of historians, archaeologists, and researchers to continue to tell this fascinating story.

Notes on Sources

Chapter 1, Running South: Artifacts from Fort Mose

Pp. 1–2, 10: The English translation of *Gracia Real de Santa Teresa de Mose* is from an informative article about Fort Mose by Jane Landers, "Gracia Real de Santa Teresa de Mose: A Free Black Town in Spanish Colonial Florida," *American Historical Review* 95, no. 1 (February 1990): 17 (notes). Information about the South Carolina fugitives and the British attack on Fort Mose is found on pages 15 and 17.

Pp. 1–6, 10: The information on these pages is from a wonderful book about the Fort Mose historical and archaeological research project. Because of the attractive design and clear text, the book is accessible to young readers: Kathleen Deagan and Darcie MacMahon, *Fort Mose: Colonial America's Black Fortress of Freedom* (Gainesville: University Press of Florida, 1995), 7–25, 32, 40–43.

P. 4, sidebar on hope and rebellion, information on the Stono uprising: Peter H. Wood, *Black Majority*, 314–15.

Pp. 7–8: "William Dunlop's Mission to St. Augustine in 1688," *South Carolina Historical and Genealogical Magazine* 24, no. 1 (January 1933): 1–23. This article contains part of Dunlop's journal and some of his personal papers from 1688 describing his voyage to Spanish Florida on behalf of the governor of the Carolina colony. Dunlop's letters to the Spanish authorities asking for return of the slaves who escaped from South Carolina in 1686 bring history to life.

P. 8, sidebar on the Seminoles: Kevin Mulroy, *Freedom on the Border* (Lubbock: Texas Tech University Press, 1993), 6–13.

P. 9, sidebar on slave laws: Seymour Drescher and Stanley L. Engerman, *A Historical Guide to World Slavery* (New York: Oxford University Press, 1998), 199, 273. *Fort Mose*, 7.

Pp. 9–10: The quotations from the South Carolina Assembly in 1719 and 1720 are from Peter H. Wood, *Black Majority* (New York: W. W. Norton and Co., 1974), 113–14 and 298.

Chapter 2, Land of the Free: History in a Ship's Log

The lists from the 1783 inspection rolls of blacks who left America with the British after the Revolution were taken from Graham Russell Hodges, ed., *The Black Loyalist Directory: African Americans in Exile after the American Revolution* (New York: Garland Publishing, 1996). This text lists all three thousand black loyalists just as they are noted and described in the original inspection rolls. According to the *Directory*, General George Washington received a copy of the lists in 1784. A photocopy of the lists can be found at the New York City Public Library, and another copy is among the holdings of the Colonial Williamsburg Library in Williamsburg, Virginia.

P. 15: *The Black Loyalist Directory*, xxii.

P. 17, sidebar on freedom with the British: Benjamin Quarles, *The Negro in the American Revolution* (Chapel Hill: University of North Carolina Press, 1991), xxiii.

Pp. 17, 19–20, 23, 25: *The Negro in the American Revolution*, 13, 23, 24, 26, 27, 31. Quarles's book thoroughly documents the experiences of black soldiers on both sides of the Revolution.

P. 22, sidebar on escape: *The Negro in the American Revolution*, 27.

P. 24: The diary excerpt on this page is from Edward Ball, *Slaves in the Family* (New York: Farrar, Straus, and Giroux, 1998), 229–30. Edward Ball, a descendant of South Carolina slave owner John Ball, who wrote the diary, has written a fascinating account of his ancestors and the people they owned.

Pp. 25–27: The excerpt from the *Memoirs of the Life of Boston King, a Black Preacher; Written by Himself, during His Residence at Kingwood School* [in England] was published in the *Methodist Magazine* (March 1798). Reproduced courtesy of the librarian and director, the John Rylands University Library of Manchester.

Chapter 3, A More Perfect Union: Learning from the Law

P. 30: Information about early laws came from two sources: Wilbur H. Siebert, *The Underground Railroad from Slavery to Freedom* (Gloucester: Peter Smith, 1968; first published in 1898), 30; and James Weldon Johnson, *Black Manhattan* (Salem: Ayer Co., 1990; reprint; first published in 1930), 7. Siebert (1866–1961), a professor of history at Ohio State University, has for many years been considered one of the foremost authorities on the Underground Railroad. Both of these books include valuable information about early laws dealing with runaway slaves.

P. 31, sidebar on a single bead: Information courtesy of Sharla Azizi, archaeologist on the National Constitution Center excavation project in Philadelphia, Pennsylvania, 2000–2002.

Pp. 31–35: W. E. B. Du Bois, *The Suppression of the African Slave-Trade* (New York: Schocken Books, 1969; first published in 1896), 21, 53, 55, 56. Excellent resource for information on the slave trade in the American colonies.

P. 32, sidebar on William Penn: John A. Garraty, ed., *The Young Reader's Companion to American History* (Boston: Houghton Mifflin, 1994), 625–26.

P. 36, sidebar on gradual emancipation: Mary Beth Norton et al., *A People and a Nation: A History of the United States* (Boston: Houghton Mifflin Co.), 161.

Pp. 36–37: John Hope Franklin, *From Slavery to Freedom* (New York: Alfred A. Knopf, 1988), 75–76.

Pp. 36–37, 39: Benjamin Quarles, *Black Abolitionists* (Oxford: Oxford University Press, 1977; reprint), 191. The scholar Benjamin Quarles has written a detailed study of the black abolitionists and their important contribution to the antislavery movement.

P. 37, chart of black population: *From Slavery to Freedom*, 80.

P. 38, sidebar on free blacks: Leon F. Litwack, *North of Slavery: The Negro in the Free States, 1790–1860* (Chicago: University of Chicago Press, 1961), 3, 14.

Pp. 40–41, narrative: John Thompson, *The Life of John Thompson, a Fugitive Slave, Written by Himself* (Worcester: John Thomas, 1856), 100.

Chapter 4, Running: The WPA Slave Narratives

The majority of the WPA slave narratives are from Norman R. Yetman, ed., *Voices from Slavery* (New York: Holt, Rinehart and Winston, 1970). This is an excellent, readable book presenting one hundred narratives of former slaves from the WPA interviews.

Pp. 43–44: Charles T. Davis and Henry Louis Gates, Jr., *The Slave's Narrative* (Oxford: Oxford Uni-versity Press, 1985), 45. An informative collection of essays critically examining the slave narrative.

Pp. 45, 47: Ira Berlin, *Remembering Slavery* (New York: New Press, 1998), 44. This is another informative collection of WPA slave narratives.

P. 46, sidebar on slave rebellions: Vincent Harding, *There Is a River: The Black Struggle for Freedom in America* (New York: Harcourt Brace Jovanovich, 1981), 66–67. William L. Andrews, Frances Smith Foster, and Trudier Harris, eds., *The Oxford Companion to African American Literature* (New York: Oxford University Press, 1997), 739. This is an excellent reference book on the history and development of the African American literary tradition, appropriate for young adults and adults. *Encarta 96 Encyclopedia* (Microsoft Corporation, 1993–95).

P. 48: *The Underground Railroad from Slavery to Freedom*, 116.

Pp. 49–50, 55: Alexia Jones Helsley and Patrick McCawley, *The Many Faces of Slavery* (Columbia: South Carolina Department of Archives and History, 1999). An interesting collection of petitions related to slavery in antebellum South Carolina from the SCDAH.

P. 51: *The Slaves' Narrative*, 40.

P. 52: *Remembering Slavery*, 55.

Pp. 58–59: John Hope Franklin and Loren Schweninger, *Runaway Slaves* (Oxford: Oxford University Press, 1999), 164–65. The authors have used court records, plantation journals, legislative records, newspapers, and other documents to analyze how enslaved men and women rebelled and escaped.

Chapter 5, Steal Away: The Enslaved Speak through Spirituals

Pp. 62–64, 67: James Weldon Johnson and J. Rosamond Johnson, *The Books of American Negro Spirituals* (New York: Viking Press, 1925), 15, 19. This book contains 122 spirituals originally published in two volumes. The prefaces written by James Weldon Johnson are enlightening essays that help us understand the context and the meaning of the spirituals.

P. 63: W. E. B. Du Bois, *The Souls of Black Folk* (New York: New American Library, 1969), 267. *The Souls of Black Folk* was originally published in 1903 and has been reprinted approximately twenty times. Du Bois (1868–1963) was an African American scholar, historian, sociologist, and leader. His book is a profound exploration of the lives, concerns, and feelings of African Americans in the early twentieth century.

Pp. 62–63: *The Oxford Companion to African American Literature*, 693–96.

P. 63, sidebar on quilts: Jacqueline L. Tobin and Raymond G. Dobard, *Hidden in Plain View: A Secret Story of Quilts and the Underground Railroad* (New York: Doubleday, 1999), 7–81. The authors investigate the possibility that quilts created by enslaved African American women might have contained signs and symbols that aided runaways in their search for freedom in the North. Deborah Hopkinson's *Sweet Clara and the Freedom Quilt* (New York: Alfred A. Knopf, 1993) is a wonderful children's story based on the premise that quilts may have been used to help runaway slaves. Even though the story is fictional, it will transport the reader back to the time of the Underground Railroad. James Ransome's striking illustrations help us to see and feel what those times might have been like.

Pp. 63–65: Scholar and theologian Wyatt Tee Walker, *Somebody's Calling My Name: Black Sacred Music and Social Change* (Valley Forge: Judson Press, 1979), 17, 56.

Pp. 65–68: *Voices from Slavery*, 53, 146.

P. 66, sidebar on the A.M.E. Church: *The Oxford Companion to African American Literature*, 12. C. Eric Lincoln and Lawrence H. Mamiya, *The Black Church in the African American Experience* (Durham: Duke University Press, 1990), 50–56.

Pp. 67, 69, 72: Arthur C. Jones, *Wade in the Water: The Wisdom of the Spirituals* (New York: Orbis Books, 1993), 106, 45, 57. A collection of spirituals.

P. 72: Booker T. Washington, *Up from Slavery* (New York: Dodd, Mead and Co., 1965), 12. Thomas Wentworth Higginson, *Army Life in a Black Regiment* (Boston: Fields, Osgood and Co., 1870), 217.

P. 73, Vinnie Brunson narrative: *Remembering Slavery*, 185.

Chapter 6, I Will Be Heard: Archaeology Meets an Oral Tradition

All of the information and material relating to the historical and archaeological findings at the Lott house in Brooklyn, New York, were provided by Christopher Riccardi, Dr. H. Arthur Bankoff, and Alyssa Lorya.

Pp. 78–80: James Driscoll, Derek M. Gray, Richard J. Hourahan, and Kathleen G. Velsor, *Angels of Deliverance: The Underground Railroad in Queens, Long Island, and Beyond* (Flushing: Queens Historical Society, 1999), 57–63, an interesting collection of articles, images, and family histories, exploring the activities of Quakers, abolitionists, free blacks, and Underground Railroad operations in Queens, New York.

P. 81: Benjamin Brawley, *Early Negro American Writers* (New York: Books for Libraries Press, 1976; original publication 1935), 123.

Pp. 81–82: David Walker, *David Walker's Appeal* (Baltimore: Black Classic Press, 1993; reprint), 91, 23. Written in four articles, this is a powerful discussion of American injustice and the need for black enlightenment.

P. 82, sidebar on Henry Highland Garnet: *The Oxford Companion to African American Literature*, 309.

P. 84, sidebar on the Missouri Compromise: *The Young Reader's Companion to American History*, 548–49.

Pp. 85–87, narrative: Thomas Smallwood, *Narrative of Thomas Smallwood Written by Himself* (Toronto: Thomas Smallwood, 1851), 38–39.

Chapter 7, "Midnight Seekers after Liberty": Anecdotes and Memories Uncover the Past

Pp. 89–101: *The Underground Railroad from Slavery to Freedom*.

P. 97: Larry Gara, *The Liberty Line* (Lexington: University of Kentucky Press, 1996), 91. In this engaging book the author looks closely at some of our beliefs and legends about the Underground Railroad.

Pp. 97–98: Levi Coffin, *Reminiscences of Levi Coffin* (Salem: Ayer Co., 1992; reprint), 20. Coffin's book, first published in 1876, is filled with anecdotes about his work on the Underground Railroad in North Carolina, Indiana, and Cincinnati.

P. 99, sidebar on trains: William Still, *The Underground Railroad* (Salem: Ayer Co., 1992; reprint), 598.

P. 101, sidebar on white abolitionists in the South: *The Underground Railroad from Slavery to Freedom*, 158–59. Stanley Harrold, *The Abolitionists and the South, 1831–1861* (Lexington: University Press of Kentucky, 1995), 68–70.

Pp. 102–8: The major source for the information on these pages is William Still's *The Underground Railroad*. Still's book, like Coffin's, is composed primarily of anecdotes; however, it also includes an interesting collection of letters and other correspondence.

P. 103, sidebar on numbers: *The Underground Railroad*, 43.

Pp. 107–8: *The Underground Railroad*, 187–88.

Pp. 108–9, narrative: From Stuart Selly Sprague, ed., *His Promised Land: The Autobiography of John P. Parker*. Copyright c 1996 by The John P. Parker Historical Society. Used by permission of W. W. Norton & Company, Inc.

Chapter 8, The Last Stop: Outrunning the Fugitive Slave Laws

P. 113, sidebar on Canadian settlements: Arlie C. Robbins, *Legacy to Buxton* (Chatham: Arlie C. Robbins and James LaVerne, 1983), 18–28, 36–41.

P. 113, sidebar on Harriet Beecher Stowe: Harriet Beecher Stowe, *A Key to Uncle Tom's Cabin* (Bedford: Applewood Books, 1998; reprint; first published in 1852), 135. The newspaper article was found in Still, *The Underground Railroad*, 248–49. *The Young Reader's Companion to American History*, 791–92. *The Oxford Companion to African American Literature*, 352–53.

Pp. 114–15: Jon Jouppien, the archaeologist who conducted the research on the Griffin home, was interviewed several times and provided the information on Enerals Griffin.

Pp. 115–18: Karolyn Smardz, "The Archaeology of the African Diaspora in Canada," Symposium, World Archaeological Congress 4, University of Cape Town, 1999. Two interviews with Karolyn Smardz. Andrew Wolfson, "Remarkable Journey Shows How Dear the Concept of Freedom Was to the Enslaved," *Courier-Journal* (Louisville, Kentucky), April 26, 2002.

Pp. 118–19: *Black Abolitionists*, 199–200.

P. 119, Information on Harriet Tubman: Sarah Bradford, *The Moses of Her People: Harriet Tubman* (New York: Citadel Press Books, 1989; reprint; first published in 1869), 1–15, 88.

P. 120: Jason H. Silverman, "Mary Ann Shadd and the Search for Equality," *Black Leaders of the Nineteenth Century* (Urbana: University of Illinois Press, 1988), 87–90.

Pp. 120–21, Gragston interview: *Remembering Slavery*, 66–70.

Chapter 9, A Mystery: When History Keeps a Secret

All of the information and material relating to the faces in the Syracuse church are from Douglas V. Armstrong and LouAnn Wurst, *"Faces" of the Past: Archaeology of an Underground Railroad Site in Syracuse, New York* (Syracuse University Archaeology Research Center, Syracuse University Archaeological Report 10, no. l, January 1998). Gary McGowan was the conservator on this project, preserving the carved faces so that they could be safely removed to the Onondaga Historical Association in Syracuse, New York.

P. 127: *The Underground Railroad from Slavery to Freedom*, 251.

P. 131: *"Faces" of the Past*, 27.

Pp. 132–35: Information about the Harriet Powell rescue is from two Syracuse newspapers: *Sunday Morning Times*, June 10, 1877; and *Post Standard*, June 13, 1953; and other clippings and reports about the rescue, courtesy of the Onondaga Historical Association, Syracuse, New York.

Pp. 135–36: Charles M. Snyder, "The Antislavery Movement in the Oswego Area," Oswego County Historical Society Publication 18 (1955), 79.

Pp. 135–37: *Black Abolitionists*, 11, 209, 210. *The Underground Railroad*, 350.

P. 137, sidebar on return to slavery: *The Boston Slave Riot and Trial of Anthony Burns* (Boston: Fetridge and Co., 1854), 1–85. A compilation of newspaper articles on the Anthony Burns trial.

Pp. 139–40, narrative: Paul Jefferson, ed., *The Travels of William Wells Brown* (New York: Markus Wiener Publishing, 1991), 35, 61–63.

P. 138, sidebar on John Brown: *The Young Reader's Companion to American History*, 112–13.

Chapter 10, The Search Continues

P. 145: *Runaway Slaves*, 295–96. *Underground Railroad* (U.S. Department of the Interior, National Park Service, Denver Service Center, Special Resource Study, 1995), 45.

P. 147: *Runaway Slaves*, 282, 367 (notes).

Additional Resources

The following resources were also among the materials used in our search for the Underground Railroad. We found these to be informative sources appropriate for adults as well as young student researchers who are interested in learning more about the people and events that are a part of this history.

Web Sites

Aboard the Underground Railroad is a Web site of the National Park Service and provides a wealth of information about Underground Railroad sites and the abolitionists who were part of this movement: *http://www.cr.nps.gov/nr/travel/underground/ugrrhome.htm.*

The Buxton National Historic Site and Museum, North Buxton, Ontario, Canada, *http://www .buxtonmuseum.com.*

HistoricCamdenCounty.com provides information about Underground Railroad activities in southern New Jersey, especially the history of the Peter Mott House and Museum in Lawnside. Peter Mott was a free black farmer who aided runaways: *http://www.historiccamdencounty.com/ccnews16.shtml.*

The National Underground Railroad Freedom Center. This Web site provides information about the Underground Railroad and the center, which is scheduled to open in Cincinnati, Ohio in 2004: *http://www.undergroundrailroad.org.*

Books

Bial, Raymond. *The Underground Railroad.* Boston: Houghton Mifflin, 1999. A photo essay with striking images related to the Underground Railroad.

Blockson, Charles. *The Underground Railroad.* New York: Prentice Hall Press, 1987. An interesting collection of narratives and stories of men and women who escaped slavery.

Chadwick, Bruce. *Traveling the Underground Railroad: A Visitor's Guide to More Than 300 Sites.* Secaucus: Carol Publishing Group, 1999. Part history and part travelog, identifying sites and museums in the United States and Canada dedicated to preserving the history of the Underground Railroad.

Haskins, Jim. *Get on Board.* New York: Scholastic, 1993. The history of the Underground Railroad from 1840 to 1860.

Levine, Ellen. *If You Traveled on the Underground Railroad.* New York: Scholastic, 1993. Good introduction to the Underground Railroad, especially for younger elementary school readers.

Middleton, Joyce Shadd, et al. *Something to Hope For: The Story of the Fugitive Slave Settlement, Buxton, Canada West.* Ontario: Buxton National Historic Site and Museum, 1999. Recounts the history of one of the largest black settlements in Canada, from its inception to the present time.

Articles

"Tracking the Underground Railroad." *Dig* (January 2003).

"The Underground Railroad." *Footsteps* (January 2003).

"The Underground Railroad and the Anitslavery Movement." *Cobblestone* (February 2003).

Videocassettes

Jubilee Singers: Sacrifice and Glory. Produced and directed by Liewellyn Smith. Written by Liewellyn Smith and Andrew Ward. PBS Home Video, 60 minutes, 2000. A very moving documentary about the Fisk University Jubilee Singers and their mission to save their school through the powerful spirituals created by enslaved Africans. A documentary that can be enjoyed by all ages.

Underground Railroad. Produced by Triage, Inc., for the History Channel, A&E Television Networks, 100 minutes, 1999. Excellent documentary on the history of the Underground Railroad and the people who were actively involved in the struggle against slavery.

Music CDs

Steal Away: Songs of the Underground Railroad. By Kim and Reggie Harris. Appleseed Recordings, 1997. This CD is a good introduction to the spirituals, especially for those who have never heard them sung. Excellent resource for the young listener.

Wade in the Water: African American Sacred Music Traditions, vols. 1–4. Conceived and compiled by Bernice Johnson Reagon. Smithsonian Folkways Recordings, Smithsonian Institution, 1996. A wonderful resource for those interested in learning about the history and development of African American religious music from the early spirituals up through contemporary gospel music.

Figure Credits

Chapter 1
Pp. 3 and 4. Thomas Jefferys map and Thomas Silver map: The P. K. Yonge Library of Florida History, George A. Smathers Libraries, University of Florida.

Chapter 2
P. 14. Map of colonies: Lars Leetaru.

P. 15. Page from ship's log: New York Public Library, Manuscripts Division, British Headquarters Papers, #14027.

P. 21. Dunmore's Proclamation: The Albert and Shirley Small Special Collections Library, University of Virginia Library.

P. 24. Cato Ramsay certificate: Nova Scotia Archives and Records Management.

Chapter 3
P. 31. Photo of bead: Sharla Azizi.

P. 32. William Penn: Library of Congress, Prints & Photographs Division #LC-USZ62-106735.

P. 38. Photos of tags: Gary McGowan.

Chapter 4
Pp. 44 and x. Frederick Douglass: Photography Collection, Miriam and Ira D. Wallach Division of Art, Prints and Photographs, The New York Public Library, Astor, Lenox and Tilden Foundations.

P. 46. Nat Turner: Library of Congress, Prints & Photographs Division #LC-USZ62-38902.

Chapter 5
P. 66. Bishops of the A.M.E. Church: Library of Congress, Prints & Photographs Division #LC-USZ62-15059.

Chapter 6
P. 76. The Lott house today: Photos by Christopher Ricciardi.

Pp. 77 and ix. Sojourner Truth: Photographs and Prints Division, Schomburg Center for Research in Black Culture, The New York Public Library, Astor, Lenox and Tilden Foundations.

P. 79. The closet at the Lott house: Photo by Christopher Ricciardi.

P. 82. Henry Highland Garnet: North Wind Picture Archives.

P. 83. William Lloyd Garrison and other abolitionist leaders: Library of Congress, Prints & Photographs Division #LC-USZ62-111195.

P. 86. Cover of *Narrative of Thomas Smallwood*: New-York Historical Society.

Chapter 7

P. 92. "Freedom Stairway": Ohio Historical Society.

P. 96. Note written by Frederick Douglass: University of Rochester, Rochester, New York.

P. 105. William Still: Print Collection, Miriam and Ira D. Wallach Division of Art, Prints and Photographs, The New York Public Library, Astor, Lenox and Tilden Foundations.

P. 107. *Escaping Slaves:* Photographs and Prints Division, Schomburg Center for Research in Black Culture, The New York Public Library, Astor, Lenox and Tilden Foundations.

Chapter 8

P. 112. Map of refugee settlements in Canada: Lars Leetaru.

P. 113. Harriet Beecher Stowe: Library of Congress, Prints & Photographs Division #LC-USZ62-10476.

P. 114. Griffin House: Hamilton Conservation Authority.

P. 115. Two lithographs: Courtesy of Tricia Borbely, the Hamilton Conservation Authority.

P. 119. Harriet Tubman: North Wind Picture Archives.

Chapter 9

P. 124. Three stone faces: Photos by Gary McGowan.

P. 127. Photo of the original church building: Onondaga Historical Association.

P. 133. Antislavery meeting: Photographs and Prints Division, Schomburg Center for Research in Black Culture, The New York Public Library, Astor, Lenox and Tilden Foundations.

P. 134. Reward poster for Harriet Powell: Onondaga Historical Association.

P. 138. John Brown: Library of Congress, Prints & Photographs Division #LC-USZ62-89569.

Chapter 10

P. 146. Wanted poster: Manigault Family Papers #484, Southern Historical Collection, Wilson Library, University of North Carolina at Chapel Hill.

P. 149. Fannie Virginia Casseopia Lawrence portrait: Photographs and Prints Division, Schomburg Center for Research in Black Culture, The New York Public Library, Astor, Lenox and Tilden Foundations.

Acknowledgments

We wish to acknowledge the help and scholarship so generously provided by the following:

Douglas Armstrong, Ph.D., Syracuse University, and LuAnn Wurst, Ph.D., State University of New York, for the archaeological interpretation and historical background of the Wesleyan Methodist Church.

Christopher Ricciardi, U.S. Army Corps of Engineers, for historical background and images, and archaeological context pertaining to the Lott house in Brooklyn, New York.

Sharla Azizi, the Artifact Research Center, for historical research and images related to Quakers and the Underground Railroad.

Karolyn E. Smardz, University of Waterloo, Department of History, for the historical background on the Blackburn family in Toronto, Canada.

Tricia Borbely, the Hamilton Conservation Authority, for her assistance in obtaining photographs of the Griffin house and related artwork.

Jon Jouppien, archaeologist, for historical background on the Griffin house, Canada.

The U.S. Department of the Interior, National Park Service, for use of their maps and related material.

The Authors

Index